THE ABYSS OF HATRED

THE ABYSS OF HATRED

JOSEPH KAMSU

Copyright © 2024 Joseph Kamsu

The moral right of the author has been asserted.

Apart from any fair dealing for the purposes of research or private study, or criticism or review, as permitted under the Copyright, Designs and Patents Act 1988, this publication may only be reproduced, stored or transmitted, in any form or by any means, with the prior permission in writing of the publishers, or in the case of reprographic reproduction in accordance with the terms of licences issued by the Copyright Licensing Agency. Enquiries concerning reproduction outside those terms should be sent to the publishers.

This is a work of fiction. Names, characters, businesses, places, events and incidents are either the products of the author's imagination or used in a fictitious manner. Any resemblance to actual persons, living or dead, or actual events is purely coincidental.

Troubador Publishing Ltd
Unit E2 Airfield Business Park,
Harrison Road, Market Harborough,
Leicestershire LE16 7UL
Tel: 0116 279 2299
Email: books@troubador.co.uk
Web: www.troubador.co.uk

ISBN 978 1 80514 218 8

British Library Cataloguing in Publication Data.
A catalogue record for this book is available from the British Library.

Printed and bound in Great Britain by 4edge Limited
Typeset in 11pt Minion Pro by Troubador Publishing Ltd, Leicester, UK

*To my wife Pascaline, to our daughters Orelia Sarah
and Mary Lyz, and to our son Christian Lazare: to their
courage in the face of the fear and mountain of difficulties
we have shared and overcome together.*

www.yhcworld.com
facebook.com/josephkamsu
Instagram/joseph_kamsu

"When you get these jobs that you have been so brilliantly trained for, just remember that your real job is that if you are free, you need to free somebody else. If you have some power, then your job is to empower somebody else."
TONI MORRISON

"Freedom is not something that anybody can be given; freedom is something people take and people are as free as they want to be."
JAMES ARTHUR BALDWIN

"I'm for truth, no matter who tells it. I'm for justice, no matter who it is for or against. I'm a human being, first and foremost, and as such I'm for whoever and whatever benefits humanity as a whole."
MALCOLM X

"A man who views the world the same at fifty as he did at twenty has wasted thirty years of his life."
MUHAMMAD ALI

1

Barbara squirms in her chair trying to free herself. The pressure on my throat increases, and my universe grows smaller and smaller; I am struggling just to breathe. With tear-filled eyes I kick, trying to hit my attacker, and desperately try to loosen the grip he has on my neck. Panic increases as I realize that this is pathetic, and my ineffective struggling may be the last thing I do on Earth.

I try to gather my remaining strength. I am about to die. Just as I regain my breath, he grabs my right wrist in a death grip; I barely have time to take in the smallest breath before he wraps one arm around my neck while with his other hand (sporting a gold Rolex on his wrist) he violently grabs my hand and rubs it against Barbara's cheek, wet with tears. Our gazes meet; she tries to say something, but she has that awful rag in her mouth. Between the tears and my dizziness, I can barely see anything. Everything feels so far away, as if I am looking at the world from the bottom of a lake. My whole being is focused on a single point: that centimeter of compressed cartilage and tissue that is preventing me from breathing. I see my death in Barbara's pupils, dilated with horror.

Suddenly the pressure on my throat ceases and I fall to my knees, greedily inhaling all the air I can. Tears are streaming down my face. I am alive. I rest my forehead on the floor and inhale hard again, then fearfully raise my head to see who did this to us. A tall man wearing a black balaclava is standing over me. It is impossible for me to identify him. I notice that the Ankh cross, the Egyptian symbol of life, hangs from the gold chain around his neck. I know this man wants to kill us, and I must stop him.

I pick up a shard of broken glass, the only weapon I can find to hit him with; however, he turns quickly and dodges my attempt to slash him. I try again, but my now-bloodstained hand is slippery, and the shard gets lodged in my palm. The killer lets out a dark, perverse laugh, grabs my arm and brutally twists it behind my back, twisting muscles and tendons, causing me excruciating pain. I bend over, trying to free myself from the pressure on my arm, but the man knees me in the stomach, winding me and causing me to fall on all fours. Wearing a pair of gloves, the maniac now approaches Barbara, wielding the pink porcelain knife I gave her as a present to carve meat. I drag myself across the floor in a desperate attempt to stop him, but his hands are quick and the blade is sharp. Barbara lets out a gasp of shock as her blood drips from the knife, splattering the floor of the room. He steps back as if to admire his handiwork, and I rush towards her to rescue her. There is so much blood! I can feel the blood pulsating between my fingers. The air becomes saturated with its iron-like smell as I desperately try to stanch the flow and keep the wound closed, but two hands grab me and drag me away. I swing my legs wildly, trying to get some kind of foothold, but he is so strong that within seconds he has already dragged me out of the room in which my friend is dying. He pushes me towards the TV and I stumble, leaving the imprint of my bloody hand on the screen. He kicks me in the lower back and my legs buckle like those of a drunk. I slam my head on the coffee table, fall back on the floor... He laughs. My skull explodes with pain; then the lights and noises around me cease and I sink into absolute darkness.

2

Three days earlier

Behind the wheel of my new Audi hybrid SUV, I have just gotten back to Milan and am on my way home when the traffic police pull me over. It is after 8pm, and there is no traffic because it is the Tuesday after Easter and many people are still away for the extra-long weekend; moreover, it is raining. My family and I have come back from a wonderful week-long vacation in Venice.

I met Flore, my beautiful and sweet wife, some 20 years ago, and we have two wonderful children: a ten-year-old boy, Kemi, and an eight-year-old girl, Naturi. I have always called Flore 'Hat', short for Hathor, after the Egyptian goddess of joy, love and motherhood, and she calls me the same: it is our affectionate, mutual nickname. As soon as our eyes met, it was love at first sight; the wings of love enveloped us and we surrendered to the feeling wholeheartedly.

Up until two years ago, on holidays we would stay home and play Monopoly, or I would entertain the children with stories about Africa, educating them about the culture of our ancestors. Sometimes we would take trips abroad, but at one point I decided to devote myself heart and soul to my career. "No more leisure and distractions," I told myself. "I must concentrate on my job!"

But ten days ago, Hat convinced me to treat myself to this vacation. Sitting in an armchair in the living room, I was reading scientific articles and studying international protocols in preparation for the competition I was to enter, when she came in to bring me a cup of hot green tea.

"Love, how is the competition prep going?" she asked, kissing me on the lips.

"There is so much stuff to study that I could go on all night," I replied, putting my hand on the pile of magazines and lecture notes stacked next to the chair.

"You are the best in your field. But you need a vacation."

"Yes, I know, only I have—"

"Why don't we go to Venice for a week? It might help you."

"Yes, but—"

"No buts."

And lo and behold, three days later, we were in Venice. We took beautiful gondola and vaporetto rides, visited museums and monuments, walked through narrow alleys and small squares and had a great time.

On the way back to Milan, we stopped only once at a restaurant on the A4 highway to get gas and eat. As we sat, we eavesdropped on the conversation three men and a woman were having at the next table: they were talking about the new Miss Italy. A black Miss Italy.

"Deep in the hearts of Italians there is always a love for the Black Venus," said one of them.

"In my opinion it was just do-goodism, just another way for people to clear their consciences. After all, if you dare to say that that girl, who may well be very beautiful, does not represent Miss Italy, they call you a racist," said another.

"What about you, Alba? What do you think?" the third man asked the woman.

"Well, she doesn't represent Italian beauty and didn't deserve to win the title," she replied.

"A *black panther* is certainly not going to solve the problem of non-EU citizens… Italians voted for her en masse, fine, but then they keep hating on the gypsies who perhaps are living in front of their building," one of them exclaimed, raising his voice. The discussion had become quite heated.

As if to belie the televised plebiscite, in Salsomaggiore the black Miss Italy of the New Era was challenged in the streets. "She is black; she is not an Italian beauty," people hissed. The prime minister had to say, during a television interview, "Italy is changing; in soccer there are black players; and so, the election of the new Miss Italy is also an important signal."

But the war continues.

Near Bergamo it is starting to rain lightly. We are already in Milan when, near Piazza Udine, a street police patrol car stops at a corner and orders us to pull over. Hat is sitting quietly next to me, and our children are playing in the backseat while the notes of *Happy*, the Pharrell Williams hit that is playing on the radio, fills the car. I turn off the music, ask the children to contain their overexuberance, and roll down the window.

The officer takes his time inspecting my new Audi. I'm reminded of a scene I saw on the news a while back: a policeman in Harrison, Arkansas (christened by the media 'The most racist city in the United States', where 95 percent of the population is white, less than one percent black, and where the Knights of the Ku Klux Klan, one of the faces the racist organization has given itself to make itself seem more presentable, has its headquarters), pulls over an African American. He takes his time approaching the driver's side while placing a hand on the butt of his gun. The 25-year-old black man has both hands on the steering wheel. The white policeman orders him to get out immediately, and the boy slowly gets out of the car. The officer spins him around, slams him against the car, and frisks him roughly. When the driver asks him why he is being treated in such a way, the policeman draws his gun and kills him on the spot.

Fortunately, we are not in America, I think to myself. We are in Milan, Italy's financial center, and, according to some, its most advanced city in many fields, including medicine.

"Is this your car?" the officer standing by the door asks me.

"Yes," I reply.

"License and registration."

I hand him the papers.

"Ben Kom," he says, reading my name. "Do you know why I stopped you?"

"No."

"Not for a traffic violation. But when I saw a black man behind the wheel, I thought you might be the car thief we've been looking for for a week. You know, an African man threatened a pharmacist in Piazzale Loreto in front of his house and stole his Mercedes. The poor guy was devastated. Didn't you see that on television? Do you know anything about it?"

Words like these can trigger violent reactions. It is up to me to decide how to deal with them. The oft-repeated, racially charged acts experienced in Italy over the past few years weigh more heavily on me than I would like to admit.

I am taller and sturdier than the policeman, and one provocation too many would be enough to set me off. Instead I remain silent, not responding.

"What do you do in Milan?" the officer asks.

"I live and work here."

"But do you have citizenship?"

"Yes."

"What do you do for a living?"

"I'm a doctor."

As if a spell has been broken, the officer changes his tune.

"I'm sorry, doctor; I won't waste any more of your time. Go ahead. Forgive my rudeness… I wish you and your family a good evening."

He hands me the papers and steps away from the door.

I start the engine again on the rain-soaked road.

Today I own a luxurious three-bedroom apartment at the beginning of Via Padova, where I live with Hat, Kemi and Naturi. I – Dr. Ben Kom, wizard of the scalpel – am deputy chief of gynecology at a well-known private hospital in downtown Milan, and I am used to fighting against the brutal and demeaning actions of social racism. I do not enjoy doing it. I have lost count of the number of legal complaints I have filed about racist threats received from unknown persons. In fact, it seems that no authority in Milan really cares.

No police officer has ever bothered to try to find out who was behind the anonymous messages I have found many times on the windshield of my Audi. Not even one policeman. Maybe what an old Italian businessman told me a long time ago, on the plane that brought me here, was true: this is not a country for everyone; people don't want to see immigrants around.

On reaching our apartment building, I see that someone has written something in red letters on the door leading to the parking garages. An overwhelming feeling of oppression takes my breath away and gives me tachycardia: "Long live white Italy. Fewer Africans and Jews; more security and wealth."

There is also a kind of caricature of my face with a cross drawn on my forehead. Hat says, "This time they have gone too far. They want us dead. I'm calling the police now."

At the thought that racists want us dead, I feel sick. I turn off the engine. My wife takes some pictures with her cell phone.

*

It is 11.30. Hat and I are watching a live debate on Rai 1 in the living room while the children are asleep in their room. We are interested in better decoding other people's ideas, and understanding why certain events have a negative impact on us.

I would not know what to call white talk-show hosts who do not accept a black Miss Italy. The appropriate term is racists. There is no black problem in Italy; there is only a white problem, and this televised babble is proving it.

"An Italian woman with black skin is not an Italian woman," says a famous journalist.

The level of discussion annoys Hat. My cell phone begins to vibrate in my breast pocket. I look at the display; it reads 'unknown'. I don't answer. My wife turns off the TV, and we find ourselves talking about our Milan, this historic city that was once, in the fourth century, the capital of the Western Empire and the leading town in the Europe of that time. In a few months, this city will allow me to fill the highly coveted position of chief of my department in the hospital.

We talk about Milan, which already at the time of St. Ambrose was culturally very lively, and was democratic in its own way. People came from all over, people who spoke foreign languages and brought their knowledge, their culture. Some of those people had great importance, not only for the culture of Milan but for all mankind. St. Augustine, for example, born in Africa, settled in Italy, first in Rome, where he lectured on rhetoric, then in Milan where he taught in a private school. One of the most beautiful passages written about the city of Milan and its generosity was written by St. Augustine, himself an African.

Back in 384, Augustine managed to secure the chair of rhetoric in Milan, where the pagan Valentinian dynasty reigned. He became a high-ranking public official and a Milanese representative of the Emperor Valentinian. He met Bishop Ambrose very often and discussed with him what makes a man a true human being, a free living being. In his constant search for that unique and life-saving truth, Augustine allowed himself to be led towards a new life by Bishop Ambrose, who baptized him in 387, officially bringing him into the Christian community. In 395, this great African himself became a bishop, and was later recognized as one of the greatest fathers of the Church.

*

About ten minutes ago, Hat went to sleep, and I am still on the couch, in the solitude of the living room, absorbed in reading an article on the complications of performing a laparoscopic hysterectomy, published in the latest issue of *TOG (The Obstetrician & Gynecologist)*. In my notebook, I am writing a list of all the absolute and relative risks, and their percentages, for this type of surgery, when I am distracted by a dull buzzing sound that reverberates in the silence of the room. It is that call again. I pick up my cell phone and see that the phone number is blocked on the display. I look at the clock: half past midnight. *Who is calling me after midnight?* I ask myself. I hesitate. Then I pick it up.

"Ben?" asks a voice I recognize.

"Barbara! How come you're calling me at this hour?"

"Good thing you answered me. I was afraid you wouldn't, the same as the other times."

"What do you want? And why are you calling me from an unknown number?"

"Sorry about what happened last week; I didn't mean to…"

The week before, in her apartment, I had found an ashtray overflowing with cigarette butts and an empty whiskey bottle on the coffee table in the living room. The TV was on. There was a picture of me on the wall. I heard the refrigerator in the kitchen close, then Barbara came sauntering into the living room to join me. Completely naked. She held a bottle of beer in each hand and reeked of alcohol. After placing the bottles on the coffee table, she tried to kiss me, but, disgusted, I put a hand on her shoulder, pushing her away. With an almost astonished look she asked me if I really didn't like her; then she dropped onto the couch with her legs spread.

Flabbergasted, I asked her what was going on. She laughed hysterically, repeatedly saying that she loved and needed me, that otherwise her life would be meaningless. I told her she was delirious, but Barbara kept calling me 'honey' and trying to hug me, repeating that she wanted to make love to me. I replied that she was so drunk she did not realize what she was saying and doing.

At one point, cloudy with alcohol, she lay down on the couch, naked as the day she was born, and I hurried to cover her with a plaid blanket resting on an armrest. At that moment, someone knocked on the door, which had been left open, and entered without waiting for an answer. It was her neighbor, a woman in her forties. I was able to slip out.

"I take no pleasure in remembering that. Just tell me what you want!"

Silence.

"What do you want, Barbara?" I repeat.

"There is someone here; he scares me, Ben."

"Who?"

"A man who wants to kill me…"

"What?"

"Ben! My life is in danger, save me… Help!"

She stops talking to me. I hear voices and noises that sound like a scuffle, and I guess that someone has snatched the phone from Barbara's hand.

I am naturally concerned for her, but also torn. A week earlier, this woman showed me, in her own way, that she loves me. What if this phone call is just another ploy to lure me back there, into her arms? But who is the man that broke into her house?

It is late. I'm in the living room alone; my wife and children are asleep. I know Hat would not be too understanding if I went to see Barbara in the middle of the night. I can't stand the idea of her worrying, or of making her jealous. I don't want to cause her the slightest bit of distress, make her unhappy, make her suffer. I love her dearly; I love her with all my being, and I have never had any crazy thoughts about other women. Who knows what problems I will face tonight? Barbara's alcoholism? A jealous lover?

I get up and, thinking that I still care about this woman, though merely as a friend, I head for the front door. I turn off the light in the hallway and leave.

3

The cab stops in front of a driveway. I pay, get out, and look over the building in front of me. Only one apartment has its lights on: Barbara's, on the third floor. It is 1.30 in the morning. The street is deserted, not a car in sight, not a sound.

My footsteps echo in the silence. The lock on the building entrance door is still broken; I don't need to buzz her on the intercom. I go in, take the elevator to the third floor, and as I near the doorway I hear a sudden crash, Barbara screaming, then a male voice and the sound of a chair sliding on the floor. After that, silence.

I mentally search for all the possible good reasons why I should not worry, imagining the embarrassment of surprising Barbara and a man in the throes of passion.

I knock on the door cautiously; no one answers. I can only hear the TV, playing music and advertisements. I try to turn the doorknob and realize that the door is not locked. In the hall and living room everything looks in order. I call Barbara. No answer. Having been there before, I know where the bedroom is; I begin to suspect that my decision to rush to her house was really absurd.

I am about to turn around and leave Barbara and her man behind when I hear a groan, followed by a loud thud and her screams, not in ecstasy but in fear! I push the door open, very worried and ready for anything.

I waste precious moments observing the horror in front of me: shards of glass on the floor; broken objects, as though there had been a furious fight; and Barbara tied up, wearing a yellow sweater, slumped on a chair. Blood drips from a deep head wound. She is white as a sheet and drenched in sweat. She looks at me, terrified, and tries to say something, but the rag stuffed in her mouth prevents her from speaking.

Suddenly I hear footsteps behind me, and immediately I am seized in a choke hold. I scream as I realize that the arm around my neck is pressing on my windpipe. I try to scratch at it, as the stranger drags me towards Barbara, but I can't. In vain I try to resist; my attacker is too strong.

4

"Ben, answer me!"

Andrea Preti's voice shakes me out of my torpor. Besides being my lawyer, he is also my friend, a sincere and kind friend, one of those people who would never stab you in the back. He was born and raised in Milan and traces his Milanese ancestry all the way back to the Sforza family. He has a law degree from La Statale, the University of Milan, and lives alone. He has been working on murder cases as a defense lawyer for some 20 years, and he always knows what to do to prove a client's innocence. We met in a university library while we were both working on our Master's theses, and have remained friends.

Today he has the difficult task of proving my innocence in court, thus resulting in me avoiding conviction.

I was arrested a week after Barbara's murder. During the restless nights I spend in the San Vittore prison, I go from sleeping to wakefulness, nightmares mixing with reality. If I doze off, I immediately wake up screaming because it feels like Barbara's warm, slippery blood is still running through my fingers. I may never be able to sleep again.

I am in the interrogation room with Andrea. I nod, but I actually don't recall the question.

"You knew that woman for about five years, didn't you?"

"What? Oh… yes," I answer distractedly.

"And you went to her home a few days ago as well, right?"

I nod again.

"Did she live with anyone?"

"I don't know."

"Have you visited her often recently?"

"Twice in the last two weeks because of her calls. Before that, it was not a habit of mine."

"Why then did you rush over to her apartment on the night of the murder?"

"I don't know. Now I almost feel like I've cheated on my wife."

My voice cracks; a knot blocks my throat. Hat has always trusted me, and she still does. But how will we explain all this to our children? They are still small, and they haven't seen their daddy in more than a week. My eyes fill with tears. What can I do?

"Tell me about that woman. How did you meet her?"

How did I meet Barbara? Through my volunteer work at the St. Francesca Romana Church Counseling Center. I have been going there on the last Thursday of every month for about ten years. I used to take the subway and get off at Porta Venezia. I would arrive around 2.30pm and would stroll around the public gardens for an hour or so before starting my shift. I really like that well-maintained park with so many trees and so much greenery everywhere, and I love to wander around its paths for a while, observing the vegetation. I would sit on a bench and watch couples kissing, people running, foreign caregivers accompanying the elderly, birds fluttering here and there. A few pigeons would come up to me to peck crumbs on the ground. When I looked up into the sky, I could see the birds perching lightly in the trees; they were joined soon after by others of their kind. Occasionally, I would catch a glimpse of a pair of feathered creatures brushing their beaks against one another, like tender lovers.

Arriving at the parish at 3.30 on the day I met Barbara, I saw that there were many immigrants waiting in line in front of the iron gate of the Counseling Center. There was a sign that specified the opening times:

Open: Tuesday – Thursday – Friday
Morning: 10am–12pm
Afternoon: 3.30pm–5.30pm

I went around the church to go in through the rear entrance, then went to the sacristy, where I retrieved the keys. Once the doors opened, the first people came in and sat in the waiting room. In the interview room, where there is a table for four people, I took forms to fill out, some informational handouts and a ballpoint pen from a cabinet, then invited the first person in the row in front of me to sit down. He was a Bolivian.

"How can I be of service to you?"

"I have been here in Italy for three months and my tourist permit has expired."

"So, you are here without a residence permit?"

"Yes, sir. And I'm looking for work."

"It is not easy to find employment without a residence permit. You know that, don't you? We can't do anything about that. Do you even have a place to sleep?"

"Yes. I live with some relatives. I just need a job. I need to work!"

"I'm sorry. I can't help you with that."

I could see the disappointment in his eyes when he got up slowly and left. Whenever I say to someone, "I'm sorry; I'm not able to help you," I feel bad; I suffer for the person I am dealing with; I feel as if I am an obstacle to his or her happiness.

I always remember that when I arrived in Italy, many years ago, at Rome's Fiumicino Airport, a policeman told me, "Boy, this is your lucky day!" Earlier, however, that same policeman had demoralized me with mean, hostile words that made me think I was in the wrong country for an immigrant. But in spite of the discomfort due to this gratuitous hostility, my mind was flying and I was repeating encouraging phrases to myself, such as this: *I am a wealthy man, a successful doctor and entrepreneur, and I keep fit with an active lifestyle, jogging and working out. As my businesses in the healthcare industry grow larger and larger and become multinational, my employees follow my business philosophy. Like a driver behind the wheel of a car with a fogged windshield, I reach out and wipe the glass with my hand, looking ever more clearly at my bright future.*

"Boy, this is your lucky day!"

The voice of the Fiumicino Airport policeman jolted me, interrupting my visualization.

"Really? I won… the lottery?"

My wobbly Italian earned me a smile and the verdict, "Don't be smart! Welcome to Italy. You can go." He concluded by stamping my green African passport with the date of entry and airport of arrival.

"Welcome to Italy," the policeman whom I had assumed to be intolerant had said. Perhaps I had misjudged him.

Once I passed that first checkpoint, I wondered: *How long does it take to get rich in this country?* One year, five, ten, twenty? I had no hope of receiving an inheritance. So, in order to get what I desired, I had to make an immediate effort to understand how the system worked. Mentally, I was trying to remember the three basic rules I had learned in my native country, now far away: first, respect for money, which implies recognizing its value, the importance of charity and the exercise of responsibility; second, control of money, through a simple system for organizing finances; and third, actually saving money, with careful management of expenditures.

Next, a Filipina lady about 40 years old entered the Counseling Center. I asked what I could do for her.

"Sir, my residence permit expires in a week, and I need a labor contract to renew it. I used to be a caregiver, but two months ago the elderly woman I was caring for died."

"I understand, ma'am."

"I have two children to support and a husband who

used to clean apartment buildings. Two years ago, when he was only 50 years old, he had a stroke, and he is now at home, disabled."

As the woman spoke, I rummaged through the pile of papers under my eyes and pulled out an employment ad.

"Ma'am, I think there is something for you. It is a request we received yesterday. A family is looking for a woman with your experience to care for a 90-year-old woman who is terminally ill. If it's OK, I'll pass on the reference and phone number."

"Yes, yes. Thank you!" she exulted.

She was very happy, and I was happy for her as well.

The next case was a Peruvian couple in their 50s, who submitted two problems to me.

"We have no home or jobs. We have been living with our friends for four years and receive food parcels from Caritas," said the husband.

"Has it been like this ever since you have been in Italy?"

"No. We always worked until a year ago, even though the money we earned wasn't enough to rent a house."

"Then what happened with the jobs?"

"We were workers in a factory, and we were fired on the spot because of the crisis."

"I see. Are you willing to be caretakers for a fancy apartment house?"

"Very willing, sir."

"Then you're in luck. I'll set up a meeting for you with the administrator of that property; hopefully you'll be hired."

"Thank you… Thank you very much!"

Seeing their faces lit up with joy, I felt relieved. We exchanged an intense look and a strong handshake; then the couple left, happy.

I continued to counsel more people. At about five o'clock a young Italian man showed up looking sick, but with a bossy attitude.

"How can I help you?"

"I need money!"

"I'm sorry but we don't give any out here."

"But I have AIDS and I have to buy medicine."

The young, skinny man – he must have been about 30 years old – was a heroin addict; his fully tattooed left arm was full of holes.

"If you are sick, all I can do is give you some addresses where they can help you."

"I don't need some shitty detox center! I just need the money, understand?" the young man repeated, looking at me harshly.

"This is not a bank."

"And you are a piece of shit! Where can I find the priest?"

"In the church, I think."

The boy glared at me, got up and left without saying goodbye.

It was almost 5.30pm when a beautiful woman came in, smiling, as I was about to arrange all the documentation in the cabinet. I motioned her to sit down. We introduced ourselves, and she, Barbara, said, "I don't have a home. I've just recently moved to Milan."

"What city did you live in before, ma'am?"

"I'm from Foggia."

"Are you married?"

"No. I'm divorced with no children. And now I'm single."

"Have you been looking for an apartment?"

"Yes. For the past three months. I work as a waitress in a café, and I don't have a lot of money…"

"I understand."

I am able to tell her that she is lucky. I have a two-room apartment for her. The owners want to rent it specifically to an Italian woman.

She is delighted. She doesn't know how to thank me. She takes my cell phone number. Later, after moving into the apartment where she is going to be murdered, she invites me to lunch to show her gratitude, because without my mediation she would never have gotten that accommodation.

*

"You told me that the first time she called you, you went to her house; she was drunk and declared her love for you, right?"

"Right."

"Okay. Your neighbor confirmed this to the police. And you loved her back?"

"I cared for her the same as for all the women I have helped…"

"Ben, I want to know if you were lovers!"

"No, no, Andrea. I never slept with Barbara."

"I see."

"Do you believe me?"

"I believe you, man. I know you're innocent."

And there's that image again: Barbara's blood running through my fingers; my hands not being able to stop it…

The lawyer is saying something else. I look up at him and try to concentrate.

"You don't remember the killer's face?"

I shake my head, no.

"He was dressed in black. I didn't even see his hair. He was tall, athletic, strong."

"Age?"

I hesitate. "I saw very little of his face because he was almost always behind me, perhaps to keep out of sight. And when I had him in front of me, tears blurred my vision. But I would say that without a doubt he was young. He was strong. Fast."

"His voice…?"

I shake my head. "He just laughed when he kicked me."

"Anything else? Whatever you can think of, Ben."

"Andrea, I desperately want to remember something to make sense out of this, but I have nothing more to add than what I told the police."

"I think that man had already been to Barbara's house, knew her, and wanted to set you up. He used the knife you had given her; he must have known where it was…"

"He could have found it in the kitchen. Every house has knives in it."

"You're right. But in any case, the investigators are convinced that you're the culprit."

"And what do you think?"

"I think he wanted to set you up, not kill you. That's my first impression. But we still have to, you know, go over all the details."

I nod and pull myself together. I feel a chill; it must be the coldness of the room. This is the first time I have been in a prison, and accused of murder to boot.

"You have to remember every detail of your life, man. Trust me, I will get you out of here," Andrea assures me, taking his leave.

I remember just a month ago I was waiting for Andrea in Piazza Duomo, which was swarming with people; many immigrants, and tourists taking pictures of the cathedral and the Galleria.

My friend arrived with his usual big, sincere smile. We used to meet occasionally to have lunch together, but that day I called him because I had some concerns to confide in him.

"Forgive the delay, Ben. I couldn't get away earlier," he apologized, shaking my hand.

"No problem. I took the opportunity to look around."

We took a seat in a restaurant in Galleria Vittorio Emanuele. The place was full. A waitress brought us the menu, and I ordered lasagna.

I had no appetite. I was too caught up in everything that was happening to me to think about food.

"Are you sure? They have luncheon specials," objected Andrea.

"I'm not hungry, but I'll eat the delicious pesto lasagna they make here," I replied.

"I'll take the special with risotto Milanese. Oh, and

bring us a bottle of red wine," Andrea said, pointing to it on the wine list.

The waitress brought the bottle of wine, poured it into our glasses and walked away. We sipped it while waiting for our orders. Andrea was talking to me about something, but I wasn't sure I understood what it was – something that had to do with a crime or murder that one of his clients was accused of.

The waitress returned with our courses and wished us bon appétit.

"Everything okay?" asked Andrea as I began to taste the lasagna.

"No, it's not good at all. I'm worried about my safety," I replied.

"Your safety? Please explain yourself better."

"Pietro Monti."

"Who is he?"

"The husband of a patient I operated on a few weeks ago. He swore to make me pay for it."

"Why?"

"After giving birth, his wife was bleeding badly and we had to remove her uterus. They will never be able to have children again and he's convinced it's all my fault."

"Did anything happen to you after that threat?"

"No, not from Mr. Monti, I think… but some strange things have been happening lately. First the racist warning on the front door of my apartment block, then a Ford Fiesta tailed me for a long time, and now my car has been set on fire."

5

15 years ago

I was not ready to face the head physician. He had summoned me to his office. I arrived at the hospital early that morning and locked myself in the doctors' office to go over all the surgical procedures our team would be using for the day's surgeries. Then I joined him, with my heart beating faster and faster as I approached his door. I found him at his desk, his arms folded, his face strangely relaxed.

"Sit down, Ben."

I could smell tragedy. I was a 30-year-old specialist, newly hired on a permanent basis through a competition, but I was still in the probationary phase, which would last six months. I was still inexperienced and was always afraid that I would not be able to handle an operating procedure as lead surgeon.

"Is there a problem, professor?"

"I want to make my message of a few days ago even clearer, to make sure you understand. I wouldn't want you to be under any illusion that you will be confirmed."

"But I am striving for…"

"You don't know operating techniques; you can't work with a team; you do not produce useful results; you are always distracted. We are not satisfied with your work!"

"Professor, I am going to—"

"There is nothing you can do, Ben. It's too late."

I lowered my head.

In the face of such a dramatic turn of events, one still has a choice: to survive or to succumb. And I had decided to survive. I would rather sell my soul to the devil than let anyone fire me. I went home and asked my wife, "Should I go to Laa'Si'?" We had been married only a very short time and wanted to wait a few years before having children.

I needed to recharge myself physically and morally. That's why I was recalling what I knew about Laa'Si'. Late one night, while watching Rai 1, I had happened upon a documentary on beliefs in Africa, and the host, after reviewing the many African peoples who practise healing rituals, had reported that in Cameroon there is a mystical community endowed with a very strong spirituality which is able to find a solution to all kinds of problems.

Before Hat fell into a deep sleep, I went to our bedroom, lay down on the bed beside her and, drawing her to me, kissed her on the neck and lips.

"Tomorrow I will call my brother Michel to get a better understanding of what I heard on television."

She lightly stroked my face without asking what I was

talking about and murmured, "Excuse me, dear; tell me tomorrow, I'm so sleepy now."

The next night, as soon as we finished making love, I got out of bed, put on my robe, and went to the bathroom. That is the place where I always find myself talking to myself, uttering motivating phrases such as, "I am healthy", "I am happy", "I like myself", looking straight into my eyes in the mirror.

Inner dialogue creates one's reality. This is the foundation of my spirituality. First I need to affirm out loud what I am, and then I need to mentally focus on it, intensely and continuously. Based on the conviction that I am what I think, I achieve in reality that which I have told myself. I always feel light and happy after I engage in this self-motivation, which I resort to especially when I have to make an important decision.

I moved closer to the mirror, which gave back to me images of roads leading to Africa and a rich and fulfilling life, which I still did not know how to reconcile with the future that awaited me because these images jarred with the current reality.

Why do I feel such a strong desire to travel? I wondered. My mind went to the funeral of my father, who, shortly after my graduation, died from a brief, lethal illness that no one had been able to diagnose. That was what forced me to return home to Cameroon for the first time.

Then, after just a year, I lost my dear mother and was forced to return to my country yet again. I loved my parents very much, even though they had their limitations, and I still carry them in my heart.

While still staring at myself in the mirror, I mentally visualized another funeral: that of my dead, rich 'father'. Once again I had to return to Cameroon.

I sank my face in my hands. I didn't want to think about it. I had to think about me now; he was fine where he was. "He loved me like a son, and I will never forget him," I told myself. Back in our room, I lay down on the bed and took refuge in my wife's arms.

"Hat, I've decided: I'm going to Cameroon."

"I'm glad you made that decision! We will go there more often in the future, including with our children when we have them, so that they can know their roots better."

"Yes of course. I will stay there ten days."

"I am convinced you will come back satisfied."

"I'll stop by the travel agency tomorrow to make reservations. I would like to leave next week."

On the scheduled day, after a six-hour flight, I landed in Douala, the economic capital of Cameroon; then I made my way to Bayangam by bus.

The fresh air infused my spirit with energy and made me feel in tune with the environment. The bus stopped at an intersection to drop off one of the 30 passengers. It was a great afternoon, clear with a mild temperature. I admired the mountainous wilderness lit by the sun.

After driving for miles over a paved road through fields and farmland, encountering very few cars on that road that wound through the highlands, the bus stopped in a clearing. I had reached my destination. I got off and retrieved my suitcase and leather shoulder bag containing gifts for the family of my older brother, who would be hosting me. He lived about a hundred kilometers from Bafang, where I was born and where our childhood home is located. He had always welcomed me warmly when I came to visit him for Dad's, Mom's and the wealthy businessman's funerals.

I walked down the narrow side street that led to Michel's house.

Compared to two years earlier, he was thinner, and his hair had gotten grayer, but overall he had not changed much. He kissed me twice on the cheeks and gave me a warm hug.

"Welcome, brother! God be praised! This is your home!"

The joy that shone through his voice warmed my heart.

"Thank you, bro."

I was happy to be back home.

We had always called each other 'bro', which is short for brother, never by our first names. This brought us closer together, even though I lived in a far-away country, and he, on the other hand, had remained an African steeped in tradition. After his escape from the seminary, Michel had decided to discontinue his studies and become a farmer.

He had prepared a hearty dinner.

"It's my wife's recipe," he said, referring to a dish I enjoyed very much.

His beloved wife Mafee had died. I had known she was ill, but I hadn't realized it was that serious.

"What exactly happened to her?" I asked.

"She had a seizure. I took her to the hospital, but nothing could be done."

"What was the diagnosis?" I wanted to know. Michel shrugged his shoulders.

"A mystery. The doctors didn't say. All I know is that it was too late to help her."

"It breaks my heart to see you without Mafee. But where are your two children?"

"One in Douala and the other in Yaoundé."

"What are they doing in the city?"

"They work there. Two years ago, right after Mafee died, they left the village. I would have liked them to get involved in the plantation but they decided to leave, saying they were not suited for this kind of work."

"I'm sorry, bro. It can't be easy for you… Tell me, what is it like? I mean the wonderful place we talked about on the phone…"

"Very spiritual. It's called Laa'Si'. I have never been there, but people in the village say there is a prophet there who teaches people to believe in themselves and succeed. Wonderful. They say those who follow his teachings succeed in building a richer, more complete life."

"What is the prophet's name?"

"I don't know… All I know is that they call him 'Great Teacher'. Some claim he preaches and performs miracles like Jesus. I have wanted to go there for years but the work on the plantation gives me no respite and I have not yet been able to find the time. When she got sick, Mafee wanted to go to him for healing prayer but unfortunately she was too tired and weak to face the long walk."

"How far is it from here?"

"More than a day's walk. It is impossible to reach by

car. Since you told me on the phone that you were looking for a place with somebody who can make you feel better and bring you abundance… well, I felt compelled to tell you that that place exists, and it is Laa'Si."

"Thank you, bro. I came here for that reason, and I'll be on my way soon, tomorrow!"

I got up at dawn and left quietly so as not to awaken my brother. As my only luggage, I carried a canvas shoulder bag with something to eat, some water and some spare clothes. I set out along the path that led to that fabulous region full of nature, where God's power was manifested to the highest degree. I had always trusted my intuition, and I was sure that I would find what I was looking for.

The day was cool but dry, and the surface of the dusty road had a firm surface, ideal for walking. Fortunately, I had gotten good workouts during my morning jogs with Hat. There was a long way to go, and my pace had to be calm and resolute.

From time to time, I would meet some friendly mountaineers who would accompany me for a stretch. When we parted, I would proceed alone, meditating, immersed in the sense of bliss that this fantastic place offered.

At noon I decided to take a break, and sat down on a flat rock protruding from the thick blanket of trees. Before I opened my bag to get my food, I raised my arms wide toward the sky to thank God. The deep, narrow valley below me was bathed in the noonday sun.

"This place is blessed. This is a blessed day. I am blessed. Thank you!" I murmured.

Having finished eating my frugal meal, I closed my eyes and inhaled slowly seven times, feeling the pure mountain air invigorate me.

I rested for half an hour, then continued on my way, my thoughts turning to Hat.

After about three hours, a large clearing opened up about ten meters from me. A hundred men and women sat in a circle there, around a strangely dressed figure in an ankle-length colorful *boubou*. They were singing a song praising God's greatness. What on earth could those people be doing in a remote place, reachable only by steep paths? There were no houses around, not even a village. Was it perhaps an open-air temple? I looked down at the stream below, glistening in the sunlight.

I slowly approached the group. I stood perfectly still and silent, waiting for the song to end and watching the man in the center of the crowd. He must have been in his forties; he was tall, slender, and radiated vitality and energy. He had youthful good looks, with a wrinkle-free face and a bright gaze. Just looking at him made me feel at peace with myself. He stared at me with a smile on his lips, radiating tenderness and generosity. He only had to bow his head and I understood that he was asking me to join the group. I sat down on the ground. A female voice broke the silence that lingered after the singing.

"I want to become a millionaire so I can change everything around me. I am a widow. My husband died, leaving me in so much debt; he ruined my life. What can I do?"

The man standing in the center of the circle replied,

"Woman, know that the only person who can ruin your life is you! Only you. Each and every one of us decides whether an experience makes them a victim or a victor. To act like a victim is to set oneself up for failure. Victims blame others, are pessimistic, lack imagination… You have a lot of debt, but you must learn to become rich, not focus on problems. From today you must be master of your emotions. Darkness does not erase darkness, only light does. After the night comes the day. To enjoy material abundance, you must have a purpose, a project you firmly believe in. It all starts with what you think and want. Your focus must be on desire, not what you lack. Ask and you shall receive. You are a spiritual force."

I heard so much wisdom in the man's words that I wondered if he was the Great Teacher I was looking for.

He answered numerous other questions.

"How can we know if an idea is the right one for the change we desire?" asked a male voice in the audience.

"Simple: if you feel joyful and happy when you think of the idea, it is right!" the mystery man replied.

After an hour of such interaction, we all stood up. From the back, I tried to make my way through the crowd to ask the teacher a few questions, but I could not reach him in time because he took a path downhill, entered the bush, and disappeared out of view. I walked further down the path that cleaved through the dense bush, but to no avail. The man seemed to have vanished into thin air.

At one point, the path branched into about ten trails. Not knowing which was the right one, I decided to turn back, and was dismayed to find that the square, which only a few minutes before had been full of people, was now deserted except for a man and a woman who were about to take one of the trails down.

I quickened my pace and shouted, "Hello! I implore you! I need help!"

The two stopped and smiled at me. After introductions, I asked them who that preacher was.

"He is one of the prophet's disciples."

"That's just where I'm going – to meet the Great Teacher. Do you know where Laa'Si' is?"

"No. We'd love to accompany you, but we've never been there and we've given up trying to get there."

"Why?"

"Friend, this is the second time in a year that we have sought that divine place, but arriving here we always find his disciple, who, after the meeting, disappears into the forest. No one knows anything about the prophet or where Laa'Si' is."

I understood that, like almost all the people at the gathering, this couple had come from afar searching for their souls, and had only encountered the disciple and this empty place. They explained to me that they had been married for five years and were unable to have children despite having had numerous treatments in the hospital, and that because they had money problems, they would like to become rich. Then, waving their hands, they invited me to look down. I leaned forward and saw in the distance almost all the participants of the gathering scattering down the mountain paths.

"We are tired of searching; we give up! And... may we give you some advice?" asked the woman.

"Sure."

"Come down with us. There is nothing up there. It's a legend invented by the people here!"

"It may be a legend," I said to myself, "but I am not the type to give up easily! Thank you for the advice. But are you really sure you don't want to accompany me?" I asked.

"No. Many have come this far, like us, and then have given up. If you climb too high, you can fall and even die."

I realized then that I had to make the ascent alone. We said our goodbyes with a hug, and they wished me luck.

I climbed up the steep mountain paths. As it began to get dark, I grew anxious that I would not make it. "This is an anxiety of a positive kind," I reassured myself as I continued to climb. Before long it was completely dark; there were no stars or moon in the sky, and there was no point in continuing if I couldn't see. I got comfortable on the ground, leaning my back against the trunk of a large tree, and relaxed to the gentle and regular hissing of the wind among the trees. I decided to climb up to the lower branches of the tree, far enough away from the ground. Fortunately I had brought a blanket. There I huddled down and tried to shelter myself as much as possible from the cold. I was in extreme discomfort. From time to time, from out of the darkness, I heard the hooting of an owl, the plaintive calls of night birds. Then, from below, came the sound of bodies rubbing against each other, of living beings snorting and breathing noisily, but I could not see what animals they were. If I had fallen, I would most likely have ended up in the jaws of a wild animal.

I attached myself firmly to my branch. After a while, I heard the animals move away and I was alone again, plunged into silence and frost. I feared that the darkness would last forever.

*

Finally, dawn came. I made sure there were no animal underneath and climbed down from the tree. I ate a piece of cake I had in my bag and drank some water from the flask, then set out along the narrow path. I was tired from the sleepless night but I walked with determination. Around noon, the vegetation thinned out and I found before me a series of fields and a striking view of some tall mountains. About an hour later, I met a mountain man who was working on a coffee plantation. He painstakingly picked only the fruits that had reached the right degree of ripeness to ensure the best quality, then separated them from foreign bodies such as stones, sticks and leaves. I knew the process: this was Arabica, much better than Robusta. The coffee would then be processed by the natural method: the fruits would be left to dry in the sun for about twenty days, and only when the skin, pulp and seeds were completely dry would they use decorticators to release the beans. The process would end with the grading of the beans according to shape and size, and then, inside containers, the 60-kilo jute bags of coffee would begin a long boat ride to Europe.

But what was a farmer doing alone on such a large, remote plantation? I was very close to reaching him when he looked up and saw me.

"Hello!" I said in a respectful tone.

"Hello, friend. Where did you come from?" he answered softly, almost in a whisper.

I observed him with keen curiosity. He resembled the prophet's disciple. He had fine features and a piercing, almost hypnotic gaze.

I introduced myself and asked, "Do you know where I can find the Great Teacher?"

"And why, man, are you looking for the prophet?" he answered, softly.

He had said 'the prophet' and not 'the Great Teacher'. I realized that I had now met another of his disciples, and immediately poured out my heart to him, revealing the reason for my journey from Italy in search of success.

The farmer remained impassive, and then, when I finished my story, said, "Everything you ask, whether small or great, if you have thought it out with strength and constancy, is understood and dealt with fully, without exception. Each question is given a corresponding answer. Every wish is granted. Every prayer is answered, every desire fulfilled. Every time you ask a question, you receive an answer."

Then he fell silent and resumed working. I did not feel like sitting idly by. Imitating him, I began to pick up the cut branches, and, each time I reached the end of a row of trees, piled them neatly. I would go back and forth while he kept expertly plucking off the dry branches and discarding them on the ground.

Suddenly, the farmer disappeared; he had abandoned the plantation. I looked around for him with a sweeping glance, then looked between the plants, shouting, "Friend, where are you?" but with no response. Total silence. Disappeared. Untraceable. After about ten minutes, I resigned myself.

Darkness came just as I was about to face the climb up a hill. Beside me was a cave, and I decided to sleep there. The next day, I knew, would be a better day. I would find Laa'Si'. They said that those who had faith would achieve success and transform their lives. I had faith and the determination to transform my life with the wealth I already had inside. "I am who I am," God said to Moses. I spoke as God, and said to myself, "I am abundance; I am love."

My mind led me to my wife. "I love you so much, and I wish you a good night!" I exclaimed out loud.

Then a memory came to mind: that of the phone that had rung on the night of my graduation, while I was in my room in the university dorms, where I was staying in Milan.

"I have bad news. Dad is dead," my brother had told me.

I felt as if I had been beaten; I was incapable of answering. Dad? How could Dad be dead?

"How did it happen?" I finally asked, stunned.

"We don't know!" answered Michel.

Dad was so generous, always smiling. He shared the little he had with those less fortunate than he. I remember that he had a pathological fear of Hell. When I was little, for one of my birthdays, he gave me a little picture of St. Michael the Archangel drawing his sword against Satan, who was lying on the ground while he crushed him with his foot. It was a strange gift because the demon was depicted with the body and face of an African. My father did not understand the implications at the time.

I did not like that gift, and I kept it under my mattress, out of sight, and not among my schoolbooks as he had asked me to do.

"You must always pray for the mercy of St. Michael the Archangel," he had advised. "This image must become your salvation!"

My dad was convinced that the only thing that mattered was reaching Heaven after death, and that I should follow that path no matter what. Unfortunately I did not agree with him; I did not like that image. So I disobeyed him.

*

I lay down in the dark cave, surrendering to the painful memories of my past, and finally, tired, I fell asleep.

Thank God it was a quiet night. I dreamed of making love to Hat. I woke up with the conviction that I was always in her heart.

Mid-morning I had a stroke of luck. I arrived at a lush green valley, yet another gift from nature. Brightly colored orchids and many other beautiful flowers danced among the trees. From afar, I could hear friendly, soft and serene voices. I kept walking for ten minutes; then I reached a clearing where there was a small village made up of many little huts amidst the flowers. All the people I met greeted me by nodding their heads. They looked incredibly young and moved purposefully, as if each had a specific goal. No one spoke; they respected the tranquility of the place by carrying out their tasks in silence.

The men wore colorful *boubou* and greeted me with smiles. They had a healthy, peaceful and satisfied air about them. The women were young and beautiful. They wore *pagne*, and their hair was natural, no extensions; some wore it in short braids. They moved through the village with amazing agility, communicating love and joy.

I could not believe my eyes. Never had I thought that, while alive, I would ever reach such a paradise where no one seemed to grow old or suffer.

"Welcome to the paradise of Laa'Si'. The prophet is waiting for you!" said a man, greeting me in a joyful voice.

"How—?"

"No questions, man. When the student is ready, the master appears!"

He silently escorted me to the Great Teacher's house: a hut full of flowers; it looked like a treasure chest that held the divine and ancient wisdom of Laa'Si'.

Slowly my companion opened the door and motioned for me to enter. I followed him inside. In the center of the room was a garden that a very young man was watering.

"Forgive me for disturbing you, Grand Master, but the *son* we have been waiting for is here."

"Are you the one whom everyone calls the prophet? The one whom everyone compares to Jesus?" I asked in amazement.

The young man nodded. "Those are your words."

"I come to you seeking advice and wisdom, a wisdom that you alone can give me."

The prophet gave me a boyish smile, looked me straight in the eye, and said, "You have asked, and you have been given the answer. Now you must allow that answer to enter your life."

Then silence. I waited for the prophet to speak again, but it did not happen.

"How can I allow—?"

"The art of allowing is in you. Go in peace, for you already know the secret," said the prophet, then he silently resumed tending the garden. I realized that the lesson was over. I left the house with my companion, who smiled again and led me to the hut where I was to spend the night.

In front of the door, he said to me: "I will send for you in two hours, at 8pm. All right?"

"OK."

I was clean because I had washed in river water on the way, so I would not waste pure water.

The experience in Laa'Si' definitely changed my life.

6

Three months ago

Gently I peel back the skin and subcutaneous tissue of the abdomen. The operation has just begun. Although fifteen years have passed, the head physician's last words have never faded from my mind: "There is nothing you can do, Ben. It's too late."

I had only been in this hospital for two months when I found myself making decisions that were fundamental to my destiny. Once I came back from Laa'Si', I was forced to overcome my fear and fight so that I would not be fired. I always wondered, however, how I would react if I found myself in the operating theater as lead surgeon. How would I behave? I used to ask myself this question during my lectures, during my training in graduate school as a gynecologist, and later, after I had won the competition for the title of medical director. When it actually happened, I reacted instinctively, as if I had been preparing my whole life for that moment.

The anesthesiologist checks the multi-parameter monitor – the blood pressure is normal and the heart rate is 70 – as I proceed with precision, speed and minimal blood loss to open the internal walls. Transverse incision of the pregnant uterus causes dark green amniotic fluid of a dense, pasty consistency to flow out copiously, preventing full view of the surgical field. "Suction!" I order as I extract the fetus. The assistant tries with the instrumentalist to suction out the meconium-stained fluid and swab the blood. Several loops of umbilical cord are constricting the infant's neck, endangering its life. I free the baby's neck to reduce asphyxia; however, the baby still remains depressed, i.e. hypotonic, does not cry, and its heart rate is less than 100 beats per minute. I turn the baby over to the midwife, who sucks meconium from its airways; then the neonatologist takes care of the endotracheal intubation, so as to bypass the lower airways and insufflate oxygen directly into the trachea. This is my second cesarean section of the night and, despite being the most difficult, it has gone well.

At the time the termination threat was made, I was convinced that my decision to wear the white coat, and my beliefs, had found their fulfillment in the effort to bring relief and hope to those suffering. I had returned to Africa, among the mountains where I was born, and where my family of origin lived, not as a doctor, but as a desperate man in search of answers. My goal was not simple: to find Laa'Si' and the solution to every problem.

I also had to recharge myself physically and morally to be able to remain on the hospital staff.

I embarked on the journey with enthusiasm, coping with the dangers, countless difficulties, and scarcity of information, because this job was so important to me.

As soon as I finish removing my bloodstained gloves, my pager goes off: another nighttime emergency. I respond. I am needed in the delivery room. I leave the operating room in a hurry.

In delivery room No. 1, the patient lying on the bed has two peripheral veins cannulated with a 14-gauge needle. She is in shock, wrapped in a reflective gold-colored aluminum emergency thermal blanket to keep warm.

Ilaria Curatola, a sturdy 50-year-old midwife, proceeds with the examination of the woman's vulva, while a young nurse assists her. I hand her the tube for the bladder catheter.

"Primary postpartum hemorrhage, doctor," Ilaria informs me as she finishes placing the pouch that is filling with urine. A trained midwife makes it easier, a lot easier, to make a diagnosis that often turns out to be the definitive one. "It seems impossible to stop it."

I adjust my protective visor in front of my eyes. Then I get the obstetric assistant to help me put on the sterile gloves.

"Would you let me take over?" I ask.

"Certainly, doctor," Ilaria replies, moving to allow me to start the procedure. The patient is having difficulty breathing.

"Four liters of oxygen per minute with facial mask," I order.

"Right away, doctor," replies the obstetric assistant.

She places the oxygen mask over the *puérpera*'s face and opens the flow of oxygen from the wall unit.

"She has lost so much blood, doctor, more than 800cc," Ilaria points out. "The birth was difficult because of prolonged labor. The most difficult of the night."

Ilaria takes the placenta and shows it to me. It has been expelled entirely; the membrane is intact. The midwife returns it to the assistant. Each gauze I apply inside the vagina is stained within moments with blood; it just keeps coming.

I check that the uterus is atonic, not contracted.

"What is the woman's name and how old is she?"

Ilaria looks at the medical record to verify the accuracy of the information. Then she looks back at me and replies, "Laura Rivera, 30 years old, *primipara*."

"Blood compatibility and coagulation tests: PT, PTT, fibrinogen, FDP, platelets?"

"Done; samples already ready for the lab."

"Good!" Systolic blood pressure should be greater than 90mmHg and diuresis greater than 30cc per hour. "One 500 ml bottle of crystalloid fluid. Let's keep two bottles of O Rh negative blood on hand. We need four more bottles of PRBCs from the transfusion center."

The midwife hangs the bottle on the hook. The contracting of the uterus should be facilitated, promoted. While simultaneously performing uterine massage, I order, "Five units of intravenous oxytocin bolus!"

"Right away, doctor."

Ilaria takes the pre-prepared syringe from the crash

cart and injects the drug very slowly into the *puérpera*'s veins while I continue massaging. Unfortunately, the bleeding is not stopping.

"Five more units!"

"Right away!"

I switch to bimanual compression, but the bleeding continues.

"Forty units of intravenous oxytocin."

The hemorrhage continues.

"Hypertensive patient?"

"Yes."

"We cannot administer ergometrine. Pass me 1,000 micrograms of misoprostol."

I insert it into the rectum, but the bleeding will not stop.

"Asthmatic patient?"

"No."

"0.5mg carboprost intramuscular."

To facilitate the contraction of the uterus, I keep massaging it and do bimanual compression. It's not working; only God could stop this hemorrhage. After spending so much time in my profession, solving complicated cases is a matter of experience.

"Has the husband been warned?"

"We have not been able to track him down. This fellow, Pietro Monti, is not answering; he has been out of Milan for a week, his wife said."

"Let's proceed with the surgery. Who knows what a blow like this will do to a couple, poor things, when they learn we have had to remove the uterus… Good thing that at least they have already had a baby."

7

The prison visiting room is located on the ground floor. The officer escorting me has the keys that open and close every door, every cell, attached to the belt of his uniform. There are a dozen or so, made of brass, heavy as hell, and they make noise with every step.

At the end of the long corridor, he opens the door to the room where there are a few plastic chairs around four small tables, also made of plastic, set up for visitors. Two inmates are conversing with two outsiders. I immediately go to the table where Hat is waiting for me. She stands up and holds me in her arms.

"Love, I miss you!"

"I miss you too, Hat," I tell her, with a long, strong hug.

"Stop that! It is forbidden!" the prison guard scolds us.

We are forced to let go of each other and sit down.

"How are Kemi and Naturi?" I ask.

"Fine. But they keep asking about you. They don't know anything about what has happened to you; they think you are on a business trip, and I prefer it that way until I find the right words to tell them the truth."

"All right. I sleep badly. But I am no murderer, Hat."

"I know, love. Who would set you up?"

"I have no idea. My lawyer is investigating."

"Your colleague, Claudio – maybe he had something to do with this?"

"No, no, no. Claudio? No. He's an ambitious guy, but I don't think he's capable of—"

"Well, he always came up with ways to irritate you. Think about the time he sent you that message on WhatsApp that said 'Black Lives Matter! Your life matters too, buddy!'"

"How can I forget that?"

That day, I didn't want to let Claudio Bianchi – who has worked in the department for fewer years than I have – know how much those stupid messages hurt me, so I didn't give him a hard time. On my mind were only my family and the goals I wanted to achieve, and I couldn't give in to taunts; stooping to his level would have been the wrong thing to do.

"If you are convicted, who benefits?"

"I don't know."

"But Claudio, love! The competition for head physician is in a month, and you two are the most qualified candidates."

"And you think he would do all this to win the competition?"

"Exactly."

I have known Claudio since college. We went to medical

school and won the residency competition together. We have been colleagues for years. He is professionally very competitive and always thinks he is superior because he is Italian and white. He is definitely the worst asshole I know, and perhaps the most disloyal colleague in the universe. He is as brilliant as I am, but his resume is significantly less rich than mine. He loves the good life and the gym, where he goes to get ripped, and he is very attached to money. The only thing we don't talk about much anymore is politics; he is a very loyal supporter of a right-wing party, though I don't know which. In short, politics is a taboo subject between us, mainly because, according to him, some men are superior and should run the world – that is, own the wealth of the planet. If I had met him today, I doubt we would have become friends. He does not tolerate losing and always gets what he wants, and he'd sell his mother to show off or become a leader.

"You may be right, Hat."

*

I think back to a few days earlier.

Around 10.30 in the morning, I hear a knock on the door of my study as I am putting on my black leather jacket, exhausted after the night shift.

"Come in," I say. Claudio enters.

"Excuse me, Ben. I know you are coming off the night shift, and it's late, but I was hoping to give you my support for what happened to you the day before yesterday," he says with a half-smile on his lips.

The air fills with his Gucci perfume. He loves luxury: he owns a Mercedes E220d SW 4matic Sport All-Terrain, a limited-edition Mont Blanc pen that he always sports, and many, many other classy items. He wears his long, silver-gray hair pulled back in a bun like a woman, and he has an arrogant countenance that irritates me. He approaches me, handing me the *Corriere della Sera*, opened to the centerfold.

"Thank you, Claudio." Another smile.

"It's the least that is possible among long-time colleagues and friends. Read it – they wrote a nice piece about you."

He does not leave, insisting, "Read it, Ben. It's a really good article!"

I lower my eyes to the paper and read: "Long live white Italy. Fewer Africans and Jews, more security and welfare.

"Dr. Kom Ben is 45 years old, born in Africa, where he lived until the age of nineteen, then moving to Italy where he studied medicine. He lives in Milan, works for a private clinic and is a highly respected and competent gynecologist.

"A caricature of his face was spray-painted on the wall outside his apartment building, along with the racist slogan 'Long live white Italy. Fewer Africans and Jews, more security and welfare.'

"There is no room for racism in our country. We cannot accept attitudes such as these – which are so dangerous for our society – being permitted and widespread. They are reminiscent of the theories, such as those on race purity, of tragic Nazi and Fascist memory, which have stained the history of mankind with blood. It is a disgrace for Milan. 'I got the chance to become Ben Kom, MD,' says the doctor. 'A chance that everyone should have.'

"The entire editorial staff warmly embraces the distinguished gynecologist. We sincerely hope he does not let it get him down, and we wish him success. – Marco Ghini."

Claudio leaves me no time to comment, and asks, pointing to the small picture hanging on the wall, "What is that, one of your voodoo rites?"

"Mind your own fucking business, Claudio."

He smiles.

"Yes, it's none of my fucking business. However, when I think about the fact that they'll have to choose between you and me for the position of head physician… I get chills!"

"May the best man win!" I snap back sharply.

"I have more right than you do, just so you know! There ought to be a law preventing a foreigner like you from getting so high up in this country!"

"You certainly are ignorant."

"Ignorant? I?"

"Yes, and so envious."

"Asshole!"

He snatches the newspaper from my hand and storms out.

I look at the embroidered canvas in the center of the wall in front of my desk. It was given to me when I was in Laa'Si', Cameroon. For a few minutes, I look it over with thoughtful fascination. The bright green background conveys an impression of strength. On the left side are depicted two musicians playing drums. They are far apart from each other; a lightning symbol suggests that they are sending each other messages. All around, the sky is clear. At the opposite end, on the right, a man is rescuing a wounded man, as if the embroiderer wanted to depict the Good Samaritan scene from the Bible. The colors in the adornment are vivid and piercing.

Are those images trying to tell me something?

*

"This cloth was made by the best embroiderer in Laa'Si', especially for you. Hang it in a place where you will be able to see it during the day because these symbols will speak to you," the woman had advised, handing it to me while everyone applauded. There were about fifty of us in a vast hall furnished with furniture made by the craftsmen of Laa'Si', at the home of the man who had accompanied me to see the Great Master. All the furnishings and kitchen utensils had also been made in Laa'Si'. On the white tablecloth stood baskets of fresh fruit and jugs filled with a locally produced wine. Our host was seated at the head of the table and had wanted me to sit next to him, to his right, which filled me with pride. After dinner, he gave me a pearl necklace that he personally fastened around my neck.

8

I first met Hat late one Thursday afternoon, about 20 years ago. She was sitting on a bench in the university garden, reading a novel about Pharaoh Ramses, and only noticed me when I was practically next to her.

I wanted to kneel in front of her and tell her how much I liked her. It was not the first time I had seen her. I had noticed her while studying in the campus library and while she was in the cafeteria or chatting with her friends at the entrance to her department. She was beautiful and always smiled. I found her determined, poised and funny. At the sight of her, I felt enveloped by a powerful instinct that heightened my imagination, and was seized by an irrepressible sexual desire. In order to win her, I would have risked my life.

I was in my tracksuit and all sweaty. When I noticed that she was sitting alone on the bench, I immediately stopped jogging and approached, trembling.

Tell her, I told myself. *Declare how you feel... No, I*

can't; she will laugh in my face. Such a beautiful girl would never agree to be with me. But desire gave me courage and strengthened my will, pushing me toward her. We were nearing the end of February.

"Hi, can you tell me what time the library closes?" I asked.

"At 7.30," she replied.

"Thank you. What book are you reading?"

"*Ramses*. It's well written. I am fascinated by the power that the goddess Hathor wields over all the characters. I'm on the last volume of the trilogy."

"Ah! What kind—?"

"I am a Pan-Africanist and I am interested in Egyptology; however I read anything that talks about Africa's glorious past."

"I read a lot too…"

"Then I suggest you read *Ramses*. You will, won't you?"

I nodded.

"Very well. I like you already," she concluded, looking at me with a gaze so tender and intense that my heart did somersaults from happiness. She was silent for a few seconds, then with a sweet smile she lowered her head to continue reading. I was standing in front of the most beautiful woman in the world, undecided what to do: leave or try to continue the conversation? I decided to walk away from her. But after a few steps I stopped and turned back.

"I hope we can continue our conversation right after I've read *Ramses*," I added.

With a sweet smile, my beloved nodded and raised her hand in a gesture of farewell.

Love changes the lives of everyone without exception. What was born between us revealed to me the secrets of my heart, multiplied my creativity, and fostered my personal enrichment. From reading the first volume of *Ramses*, I understood that the goddess Hathor infused love into the hearts of men to enable them to break down the walls of hatred and build bridges of good will. I now knew that any person I met could be the goddess Hathor, to whom I could simply say, "I love you," silently and with a smile on my face. I understood that love makes the eyes shine, smooths the forehead and fills the mind with positive thoughts. Who can deny the change we undergo when we are in love? I had promised the one I already considered my woman to read *Ramses*, and after only three days I was halfway through the second volume. I felt happy. Loneliness bored me. I had built a dam on the river to stop its water, at least temporarily, but the water was finding its way through. For three years I had substituted study for sexual desire, not seeing any women; but from the day my eyes fell on Hat, I felt the need to express my sexuality physically.

As I had hoped, on the third day I found her sitting on the same bench as before. She looked even more beautiful to me, dressed in a pair of jeans and a cotton shirt. She looked healthy and calm.

"Hello, friend," she exclaimed warmly.

"Hello…"

"Sit next to me."

As I took a seat next to my beloved, I could not help but notice the precious chain with a cross on it that she wore around her neck.

"It is very beautiful. Are you a Catholic?"

"Yes, I am a believer," she replied, rubbing the cross between her thumb and forefinger. "Do you have anything to tell me?"

"Yes, we have many things to talk about."

"Then let's start."

"Today, after studying, I finished reading the second volume of *Ramses* just to have an excuse to see you." I immediately began to relate to her the things I had learned about the power of the goddess Hathor, and how love gives nothing but itself.

"The power of love consists in making us free, not in possessiveness nor in being possessed. True love is not obsession, because a person obsessed with love is like an addict who loses control of their rational faculties and volition, and acts in a distorted, disorganized and destructive way," she said.

In *Ramses*, obsessive love was said to generate jealousy, a feeling that can drive a man mad by turning him into a beast, and even lead him to kill.

By now the two of us had broken the ice, and we talked for hours about love, sex, romance, marriage, God – no topic seemed too bold.

"Why do married couples quarrel?" I asked.

"You know, Hat, couples often fight for futile reasons," she said.

"Hat? But… who is Hat?"

"Sorry, I just felt like calling you that, after the goddess Hathor. Don't you like it?" she replied.

We burst out laughing. That nickname, derived

from Hathor, suited me just fine. Very well indeed. I was flattered by it. I began to realize that the romance I had so vaguely fantasized about was coming to fruition.

"I bet you'd like me to call you Hat, too."

"That's right," she replied. Then for a long moment she stared into my eyes.

So, we started dating. We were so good together that not long afterwards I decided to take the plunge.

"Hat… will you marry me?" I asked her one night while we were having dinner at an African restaurant. There were few people there. We had been assigned a seat at the back of the room. We were seated across from each other. The waitress brought us a teapot; when she moved away, I slowly poured the tea into my beloved's cup.

She stood, looking at me in silence, then answered, "Our story is so—"

I interrupted her. "Please say yes. I truly love you… I will love you all my life. Tell me you love me too!"

"From the first moment I saw you, my heart told me that you are the man of my life. I would like to marry you right away, Hat…" There, that was the magic sentence I was waiting for. "But it is clearly not possible now. I am preparing my dissertation in molecular biology, and you are going to get your medical degree in a year and a half. Hat, this is a very important decision. All I ask is that you wait two years. You have to finish your studies first!"

"Two years seems like an eternity to me. But that's OK; I understand."

I looked at her and saw that she was keeping her eyes closed, as if she was dialoguing with herself to find the right words, which she finally uttered with great tenderness. "I would like to fall asleep every night next to you, and in the daytime always be in your sweet company."

We stayed and chatted until the restaurant closed, then walked to the women's dorms. She kissed me on the mouth, and with my eyes I accompanied her until she entered.

I arrived home at midnight. I slipped happily into bed, and before I closed my eyes, I said to myself several times, "I love you, Hat; you are the light of my life…"

We lived our love passionately, ardently, with great sexual understanding. We were happy, in a state of grace that bordered on spirituality.

9

I walk into the prison mess hall. As soon as they see me, the other inmates suddenly stop talking and look at me, following my every move.

"Look, friends, there's the killer doctor!" shouts an energetic man with a large Christian cross tattooed on his neck. "What a piece of shit!"

I avoid answering this dickhead. From my first day in prison, the guards warned me, "He's completely out of his mind. You never know how he might react, that psycho. He's capable of killing you for nothing. He hates Africans."

I take the tray and look for something edible among the foods displayed behind the display case. There is nothing that even vaguely resembles the fine dishes my wife Hat prepares.

"Dr. Kom, today for dinner we have pastina in broth, mashed potatoes and ham. Then a fruit, your choice of an apple, a pear or an orange," says Miriam, the young woman serving behind the counter.

I set the tray down on a table for eight, take a seat, and start eating. Four other inmates also sit down, and soon afterwards, a short African man in his fifties. We have seen each other before, here in the cafeteria, in the gymnasium and in the yard, but this is the first time he has approached me.

"Good morning!" he greets me in a French accent, before adding, "You don't mind if I join you, do you?" He takes a seat opposite me while the other four, busy eating, do not open their mouths.

"Of course," I reply. "*Je m'appelle Ben. Et vous?*"

"Diouf Sall," he replies with a polite smile. "*Ah, bien, vous parlez français!*"

"*Oui!*"

"*Ivoirien?*"

"*Non.*"

"*Camerounais?*"

"*Oui.*"

"*Très bien. Je suis Sénégalais.* I am from Dakar, and I have been living in Italy for 30 years now. I arrived here illegally by boat in Lampedusa."

"Ah, I see."

He gives me another friendly smile. "And how did you get into this country?"

"By air, in a conventional way, 25 years ago," I reply.

"Strange life! I am in prison with an educated brother, a doctor who, until yesterday, was saving lives! Do you realize? You know, I never went to school… Many years ago, every morning at dawn, they used to load me into a van overloaded with laborers traveling on Highway 16 to

Lesina, Puglia; it had eight seats, and there were 14 of us on board, all Africans from Morocco, Nigeria, Gambia, Ghana, Senegal, Mali. Only the driver was Bulgarian. I was earning 20 euros a day for picking tomatoes. Then I moved up to Milan 15 years ago to earn more and I found myself in the drug-dealing business. One day the police stopped me. They had been tailing me for some time. They found 20 grams of crack inside a cell phone case hidden in a drawer and arrested me for possession and dealing drugs."

"Have you been in jail ever since?"

"Not exactly. I have been in and out several times for the same offense. Unfortunately, two years ago I was arrested and sentenced to 20 years for manslaughter and dealing because I had sold ecstasy pills at a disco to a 22-year-old girl who later died. I think they bewitched me with a *mamiwata*, the evil spirit. I am convinced that someone in Africa wants to ruin me. I am not a bad person, but they never wanted me, don't want me, and will never love me in this fucking country."

As Diouf narrates, believing what he wants to believe, what he needs to believe, I understand that truth is elusive, hiding in our blind spots, our preconceptions, our hearts, and we must try to see it.

Many years ago, when I was in college, I used to attend lectures that the Buddhist Students' Association held on the university campus. Their spiritual teachers argued that human beings have free will and the faculty to distinguish good from evil, and that the most important things are mindfulness and meditation to achieve nirvana–liberation from the cycle of births and rebirths.

"Perhaps we should not put too much faith in a *mamiwata*, brother. After all, the wind of life blows in the direction and at the intensity we want it to blow."

"But life is unfair. Believe me, doctor, I have always prayed to Allah five times a day, and with what result? Ending up poor and in jail! This world sucks!"

"Okay! Let me tell you this: the Creator has put into every creature a fragment of himself, a light, a spark, some of his very spirit. And thanks to this spirit, every creature can become a creator. This means that human beings should not wait for an outside source to solve their problems, but work hard, with thought and action, to get what they need."

"Gee, doctor, but are you a doctor or a preacher? If your Creator is so all-powerful, why are you in prison now? Did you want to kill that poor woman so badly in order to end up locked up here? You piece of shit!"

"That's not true; I didn't kill Barbara!"

"Liar!"

"Believe me, brother, I would not be able to—"

Diouf gets up and leaves the table.

"It was a pleasure to meet you," he hisses. "Bastard!"

10

In San Vittore there is a kind of central square, called the Rotunda, with the various cell block wings branching off. In March 2017, during his visit to Milan, Pope Francis met the inmates and shook their hands.

A small staircase leads to the first cell block, also called 'the penal section', where 'young adult' inmates, who are between the ages of 18 and 25, are locked up. It is the block that prison police consider the most complicated because it is home to boys who have often committed violent or drug-related crimes. They are divided into gangs, especially the South Americans, and all it takes is one silly incident to set off their rabid tempers. They come from difficult pasts, from very complicated lives; many are awaiting trial. All the main offices, such as the interview room, the command office, the lawyers' and magistrates' room, and the various medical clinics (psychiatry, X-ray, etc.) are located on the second floor.

The second and fourth cell blocks are unusable. The

third cell block houses inmates with drug problems. They make up 30 percent of San Vittore's prison population. Most are already undergoing drug treatment; they are addicted to heroin.

In the sixth block are the maximum-security cells, where the inmates who have committed the most serious crimes serve their sentences. When it comes to crimes against women and children, the other inmates want nothing to do with them, so they are better off separated. An unreal silence reigns in that section.

When I first arrived at San Vittore prison, I underwent a preliminary examination to determine my mental and physical health status. In fact, psychiatric disorders are manifested by more than half the inmates, and that's not even counting drug problems. After this process was finished, I was assigned to the fifth block, the block designated for new arrivals. Here you will find chaplains' offices, an infirmary (each block has its own), a barber shop, a library, various offices for those working in that block, classrooms for those who attend the in-house school, and an ample outdoor space to get some fresh air. There is also a soccer field.

Here, besides having showers, the cells only sleep two people, plus there is a gymnasium and a small room where you can play ping-pong or cards or watch television. Our cells are lined up on both sides of a wide central corridor. The bathrooms are in a separate room. In addition to bars, the windows also have a narrow mesh screen.

The cell where I was put, which has a television set, was not chosen, as is usually the case, by the block inspector, who knows from experience and professionalism whom to put in a cell with whom in order to avoid fights and other problems, but by the prison warden himself, who received me to find out what I wanted and how I felt. I am a respectable man, a respected professional who has never been in trouble with the justice system, and suddenly, presumably shocked, I found myself in San Vittore.

My roommate is snoring deeply and cavernously, as he does every night. He is 40 years old and has been here for more than five years for several robberies, burglaries, and a couple of armed assaults.

The first time I entered our cell, I greeted him and asked his name, and he said, "It is my fucking business."

I was baffled for a few seconds, then proceeded to ask him questions such as, "What is life like in here?" and "What are the other prisoners like?" and "Excuse me for calling you by your first name. Do you have a family? A wife? Children?" and so on for a couple of days. On the third day he exhibited a half-smile under his arrogant, villain air. In the end, we talked all night about our predicaments, and finally began a relationship based on mutual respect.

I am lying on the mattress and looking at the ceiling, tormented, as usual, by insomnia. I am innocent, but that does not guarantee that I will not be convicted. I wonder how Andrea will prove my innocence. How long will I have to stay here? Will I be able to save my reputation?

I try to direct my thoughts towards something positive, to draw on my strength and determination, qualities that have enabled me to overcome so many difficulties. I focus on the past, when, at the beginning of my career, I had feared I would fail.

11

"What happened the morning after Laura Rivera's hysterectomy surgery?" the lawyer asks.

We are in the interrogation room. I begin telling my story, and he listens patiently.

Early that day, I was in the lobby with the usual bustle of patients, relatives, doctors and nurses. The café was crowded; the delicious smell of brioches and cakes, mixed with the smell of coffee, hovered in the air. I greeted my colleagues, then paid and got my receipt for a coffee at the cash register. Meanwhile, I wondered if Mrs. Rivera would feel better soon, and if she had accepted the fact that she could no longer have children.

"Doctor, your coffee," said the barista, an African girl in her 20s with a very pretty face. As I drank my coffee, a man in his 40s came in, gray-haired, tall, obese, with a big nose.

"We have lost everything because of you!" he bellowed.

"Excuse me; do I know you?" I asked, placing the cup on the counter.

"I'm Pietro Monti, and you have ruined my wife!"

"I'm sorry. There was nothing else we could do. Your wife was hemorrhaging. It was a matter of life or death. In those situations, you have to remove the uterus."

"I'll kill you, you son of a bitch!"

"Calm down…"

"I hate people like you who can't do their jobs."

"I won't let you insult me like that."

"Shut up, you incompetent pain in the ass!"

"Look, Mr. Monti, stop insulting me. I'm sorry about what happened to your wife, but complications due to childbirth left us no choice but to—"

"Sterilize my wife! And without our consent!"

"Such an emergency does not require consent. I acted according to my conscience because it was a choice between letting your wife die or saving her. I chose to save her. I did not need consent."

"Asshole! Just listening to you makes me want to put a hole in your head!"

"Please calm down, please calm down. No one wanted to sterilize your wife."

"Oh no? And what did you want to do?"

"As I just told you, it was a choice between life and death."

"Shut up! I swear I'll make you pay, and I always keep my promises! You bastard! Fucking African!"

*

"What a shitty person! Ben, do you remember the

case of that Nigerian, Emmanuel Chidi Namdi, beaten to a pulp in the summer of 2016 for trying to defend his wife, who had been called 'an African monkey'?"

"Yes, the newspapers called it manslaughter."

"That's right. Do you also remember the African migrant who was gunned down a year ago not far from Castello Sforzesco?"

"Yes. The incident is still being investigated by the Carabinieri."

"A couple of shell casings were found near the corpse. The far right is behind these two murders."

"And do you think Barbara's killer might be a militant neo-Nazi?"

"I will have more information when I talk to the policemen. I did find out, however, that Mr. Pietro Monti is the Milanese secretary of one of those far-right groups, and he uses his own ideas marked by racial hatred in his propaganda. Some time ago, someone from his organization hung a banner at the Turin stadium with a phrase written in black paint with the words 'Mario' and 'African' highlighted in red to form the phrase 'African Mario.' Special Operations Police proved that the word 'African' was being used in a derogatory manner."

"Do you think Pietro Monti is behind this murder?"

"I don't know. I'm working on that lead. But we also have to let the police do their job. We will catch the killer, Ben."

"I thank you, my friend."

"I will come back to see you as soon as I have any news. And I hope to have some soon. I have to run now – I'm going to see the chief inspector in charge of our case."

12

Almost every morning except Saturdays, Sundays and holidays, between eight o'clock and ten o'clock, we physicians in the department get together in the meeting room for the shift handover.

The chief physician retired a month ago, and I, who was deputy chief for a few years, have been appointed acting chief until the official competition, which is scheduled for next month. For now, I have all the responsibilities of the department on my shoulders.

The goal of a lifetime. At last I can have some hope of becoming, at only 45, one of the luminaries of Italian medicine, an authority on obstetrics and gynecology, with a list of scientific publications as long as the phone book of a provincial town. It is time for me to go down in history, and I am determined to work hard to achieve results never seen before.

At the end of my difficult night on call, almost around the time of shift handover, I am called back to the delivery room for an emergency, and decide to give a lecture as well.

Among the four women in labor, there is one with fetal dystocia. This is a 42-year-old, obese, first-time mother. Shoulder dystocia is evident: the fetal head shows in the perineum, but appears to be pulling back in tightly against it; this is what we call 'the turtle sign'.

I turn to the head nurse. "Chiara, let's start the maneuvers to dislodge the anterior shoulder."

"I'm ready, doctor."

"All right; great. Let's proceed with the McRoberts maneuver."

The woman's thighs are hyperflexed by Chiara and two nurses called in for support.

"Perfect." I tell the students, "This is a rare case. Mark down all the steps in the procedure. The first thing you do in case of shoulder dystocia is to call in additional staff for support. Then, you use the McRoberts maneuver to increase the size of the pelvic outlet."

As Chiara applies suprapubic pressure to encourage rotation and dislodgement of the anterior shoulder, I continue my explanation.

"Bottom pressure should be avoided because it can worsen the situation or cause uterine rupture."

I insert my right hand into the back of the vagina and push on the posterior shoulder to rotate the fetus in the direction that is most comfortable, then ask, "What's this maneuver called?"

Silence.

"Guys, don't be afraid to make mistakes. Be brave, step up!"

Three medical students and a resident are in the room, while the head nurse, three nurses and I, wearing scrubs, masks, overshoes and gloves, are attending to the woman giving birth.

"Wood's maneuver," I say.

My hand flexes the fetus' posterior elbow, and I rotate the fetus' arm and hand across its chest to free the entire posterior arm.

A student raises her hand. "When is an episiotomy used?"

"The maneuver I just did increases the risk of fracture of the humerus or clavicle. Sometimes the clavicle is intentionally fractured at a point away from the fetal lung in order to dislodge the shoulder. Then, an episiotomy can be performed at any time to facilitate the maneuvers. Do any of you know what the Zavanelli maneuver is?"

A student with a beard promptly replies, "If all maneuvers are ineffective, the obstetrician flexes the infant's head and reverses the cardinal movements of labor, bringing the fetal head back into the vagina or uterus again."

"What do you do at this point?" I ask.

Three students start to answer, but the bearded one beats them to the punch.

"The fetus is delivered by cesarean section."

"That's right. And congratulations: you are the first student to demonstrate knowledge of the maneuvers for shoulder dystocia," I say, hiding my smile behind the surgical mask. "You're good! What are the risk factors?"

A student wearing a hijab replies, "They include: fetal

macrosomia, maternal obesity, maternal diabetes mellitus, prior shoulder dystocia, operative vaginal delivery, rapid delivery, prolonged labor."

"That's right. With shoulder dystocia, the risks of morbidity – for example, brachial plexus injuries and bone fractures – and of neonatal mortality also increase."

13

It is late afternoon, and it is already dark outside.

"I have to be strong."

After all, I'm here and I don't seem to have any real alternatives, since I'm in prison on a murder charge.

"Don't worry, Ben. We're doing everything we can."

That statement is the first thing I remember when I think back to the moment when I woke up after the attack at Barbara's house. Those were the words of the nurse who was watching me carefully, as if she was looking for a reaction from me. I was on a stretcher in the hospital, in the Urgent Cases section of the Emergency Department. I was in a lot of pain. Doctors and paramedics were doing their best to save me. The strange thing was that someone – my attacker, I suppose – had contacted the police, who recorded the call at 2am. A robotic voice, perhaps distorted by an electronic device, called for a patrol car to be sent to Barbara's apartment. When the operator asked the reason for the emergency, the voice replied that a man had killed a woman in her home. When asked to provide contact information, the anonymous caller hung up.

Nevertheless, the operator decided to send officers to the scene; they then called 118 for an ambulance.

The killer had decided that I was meant to live and Barbara was meant to die. He had knocked me unconscious, and once I woke up in the hospital my whole being was fighting to survive. My pulse rate was 220 beats per minute. In the medical chart they had written 'severe concussion'. My eyes were wide open, with a fixed stare. They administered a strong sedative. I realized my life was in danger. Fortunately, tests showed no internal damage or bleeding on the brain. My brains, fortunately I would say, were not fried! That same night, emergency room staff tracked down Hat, who rushed to the hospital by herself, leaving the children at home with the babysitter.

"My love... Thank goodness you are alive, my love!" my wife exclaimed emotionally when she saw me. I was very happy to see her again.

"I'm so sorry, honey! I didn't want to do all this to you. I never cheated on you and..."

"I know. I trust you, and I know you are innocent."

"Thank you, Hat. How are Kemi and Naturi?"

"Fine. They don't know anything yet, and it's better that way for now. You just take care of yourself and you'll see that we'll find a way to fix everything."

Only six hours after my arrival in the emergency room, when I was still very debilitated and in pain, two police officers showed up at my bedside.

"Who are you?" I asked.

"I am Inspector Trebano and this is Deputy Inspector Rocco." They explained that the case had been assigned to them.

"Have you found the murderer?" I wanted to know. I had no idea at that moment that they were thinking it was I who had killed Barbara.

"What happened?" asked Trebano, cutting me short. They questioned me for more than two hours, and I told them what had happened. Then they came back the next day, and after another round of questioning, they asked me bluntly if I had by any chance killed Barbara. That accusation outraged me. I shouted, professing my innocence; the last thing I expected was to be accused of murder. I was told that the victim had fought fiercely against her attacker; the chaos the apartment was found in proved it. I protested that the murderer had tried to strangle me; I could have died too. I showed them the marks on my neck.

But the two officers didn't seem to care. It was useless. I was unable to prove there was another man in the house that night. I called for Andrea, who came to the hospital. My lawyer said the police allegations were only circumstantial and not based on concrete evidence. He wanted to examine the crime scene.

The next day Andrea came to see me. He said the room had been ransacked, but forensics had only found my fingerprints all over the apartment, in addition to the victim's, of course. The floor was smeared with blood. The most important piece of evidence seemed to be the knife with my bloody prints on it. After six days in the hospital,

I was discharged, but my lawyer could not stop the police from escorting me to San Vittore, where I was to be locked up pending trial. This was because the magistrate, deeming me a flight risk and ruling that there was a risk of evidence contamination, signed an order for my incarceration.

Who was the stranger with the robotic voice? It sure as hell was not I. I was innocent, but the police said that the call came from a phone found at the crime scene which was registered in my name. How could that have happened? It was obvious that the real culprit, after committing his horrendous crime, had scattered clues all over the house and called the police with a device registered in my name in order to frame me. It did not make any sense. Even though they found me unconscious and bleeding, lying next to the victim, they were still accusing me of murder?

"I have to be strong," I keep telling myself.

I'm sitting with other inmates in the light-gray, white-walled TV room. My chair is a little further back than Diouf's and the other five inmates', so I can see both them and the flat-screen television. They are showing a prime-time talk show. The chairs are dark, apparently indestructible, and cold, in keeping with the walls and my thoughts.

"We must fight poverty in Africa," says the host, striving to maintain a neutral expression. Images of humanitarian operations carried out by Italian volunteers in Africa scroll across the screen. Sitting next to the reporter is a very famous Italian actress, patron of the campaign, who promotes the importance of solidarity with Africans, and meanwhile the words SAVE AFRICA scroll along the screen.

As the SAVE AFRICA ambassador talks about her NGO, I think back to Don Pietro, the founder of the Christian community that welcomed me when I arrived in Italy. He too had a vocation to fight poverty in Africa. There is a flood of people ready to fight for the happiness of the poor African. NGOs spring up like mushrooms and invade mass media and advertising space, wanting to save Africans from misery at all costs. They take it upon themselves to organize events and rallies to raise money on behalf of Africans.

In front of an audience of wealthy Italians, with microphone in hand, a leader of Don Pietro's community welcomed us African guests, and called us to the stage one by one. Intrigued faces devoured us with eager eyes. They wanted the show to begin. And we, with smiles on our faces, entertained them with songs and dances from Africa. During the intermission, Don Pietro, concerned fundamentally about the money we could raise in the form of donations, took the floor and insisted on the concept of solidarity.

"Here are our Africans!" he harangued the audience. "They need our support…"

The second half of the show was funnier; our stories made people laugh. And, strangely enough, the more upsetting they were, the more applause we received. We didn't like to always talk about Africa as a tragic and unhappy island, a world alien to civilization, full of Islamic bandits and terrorists, epidemics and beggars. But, during the rehearsal evenings, Don Pietro would insist on what was best to say and do to stimulate the generosity of the audience, demanding outstanding, flawless and moving performances from us.

"I want misery!" he would say. "You have to look pained to strike the donors' sensibilities."

I noticed that the more destitute we looked, the more our 'benefactors' convinced themselves that they were superior, privileged people. My friends and I were far from happy to play these sleazy, petty roles, but unfortunately we felt obliged to pretend that we were happy to demean ourselves in order to be worthy of the bread and shelter that Don Pietro offered us.

In that community, we only existed through tragic events, and we had to portray ourselves as different from others. Unfortunately, even I, the beloved son of a father who had sacrificed himself for me and my brothers and sisters, was on stage, in front of strangers, lamenting how unfortunate it was to live in Africa, a continent in need of new horizons... In short – and this was truly mind-boggling – I had to conjure up sinister situations that I had seen only on Western television!

"How do I see the future of Africans? I see that we have no future unless you help us!" The applause that followed was so prolonged that I felt like a star. I felt horribly at fault but, after all, I was there precisely so that I could help change all that.

The virtues of sobriety and frugality were completely absent in Don Pietro's community. He had reserved for us an important role in the profitable activities of the center, and the business thrived. Another splendid residence was being built on the vast property, an impressive glass and steel building with marble floors and satellite dishes towering on the roof.

"We struggle against poverty in Africa."

A subtly subservient atmosphere reigned in the center. The curtainless window in my bedroom looked out on a beautiful landscape, as peaceful as a celestial painter's painting in which time stood still. I did not have much room for furniture other than a bed, a bedside table, on which rested a lamp, a small closet and a mirror over the sink. No television, no desk or chairs, no telephone, no books or Bible; only a wooden crucifix adorned the ochre walls. The communal shower and toilets were located down the hallway on the second floor.

*

I shake off my memories and go back to watching the talk show on TV. I am again submerged in the pool of detainees, who, like me, are sitting on cold chairs watching that flat screen in search of some connection with reality.

The SAVE AFRICA ambassador gets up and leaves the presenter, who announces an interview with an Italian politician, who smiles, sighs, and says, "I have been using public transportation in Milan for 20 years, and I think, given the arrogance, rudeness, and violence that reigns there, that just as there used to be seats reserved for veterans, invalids and pregnant women, at this rate we will have to establish seats or carriages exclusively for the Milanese and decent people. If we don't put a limit on immigration, that is what it will come to. The needy people are not those who arrive in Lampedusa and are disinfected; the needy people are the citizens of Lampedusa and Bergamo, who are then robbed by those who have been disinfected."

"You asshole," mutters Diouf in irritation at the address of said politician, who never stops blustering about the fight against immigrants. He not only speaks with disdain about the people landing in Lampedusa, but refers to Africans as 'those people' who want to overrun the Beautiful Land with terrorism. His words pierce my eardrums and make me feel dizzy. I really want to leave, but in the end I decide not to. I take a deep breath, close my eyes and think about all the things that have gone wrong, the many dead ends my life has taken, the wrong decisions I have made. Some people call it fate. I don't believe in fate. I am a fairly rational person. Life is about choices and consequences. But who could have foreseen that one day I would find myself here, sitting with a drug dealer and convicted felons in the TV room of a prison, waiting for my lawyer to put together enough evidence to clear me of a damning charge?

As the politician lays out his hard line against the landings in Lampedusa, I cannot help but think back to when, at just 19 years of age, I purchased an economy class seat on a flight to Italy. I was sitting by the window next to an elderly Italian man, who at first would not answer my questions; he had mostly just scrutinized me, a bit like looking at an unfamiliar and exotic animal in a zoo. By the end of the journey, however, he opened up and told me that in order to succeed in life, one must possess determination, strategy and a willingness to work.

"I understand," I replied.

The sincere smile on his face encouraged me to continue our conversation. We talked about many things, about my plans and my hopes of becoming 'a billionaire like Berlusconi'.

"Don't dream too much, boy. In my country things are more complicated than you can ever imagine. You work your ass off and someone else gets the credit."

"Ah! But in Italy you can get rich, right?"

"Take it easy; don't be so optimistic!"

"But I have the ability—"

"It's not about being capable. To put it simply, as I said, someone else gets the credit. I have 50 years' experience as an entrepreneur in my country."

"So, it really is not possible to succeed?"

"Don't you trust me, boy?"

"Well, yes… but is it an advanced country, or isn't it?"

"Advanced to a certain extent. It's not America."

"But the economy is strong… I want to change my life in Italy. Will that be possible?"

"One step at a time; first, let's see how you are welcomed."

"Why don't you tell me the truth?"

"You know what, boy? In Italy the real power is held by politicians, and so many of them are racists," the entrepreneur finally said. I am not a pessimist, nor am I a skeptic or someone who gets depressed easily, but at that very moment I realized that to achieve success I would have to fight against injustice and racism.

The captain had announced that the plane would be

landing on time in Rome. Through the window, I could see the Eternal City getting closer and closer.

The landing was smooth, the weather was clear, and it was a pleasant 25 degrees.

Then, at passport control, the wait began.

Ten. Thirty. Sixty. Ninety minutes. My turn never seemed to come. I looked around. Almost all the European maroon passports were returned to their owners after a quick examination by smiling, helpful policemen, often without even looking the travelers in the face. The green African ones were examined last, with an exasperating slowness; it seemed like something purposely done to make us non-Europeans nervous. For what reason? I did not know, but strangely I did not feel agitated even though the police had arrested five African travelers on the same flight as me before my very eyes. Who knows what crime they had committed – illegal immigration or drug trafficking?

I didn't know and didn't care to know. I had nothing to hide, so I was not afraid.

I had a regular visa, which was issued by the Italian embassy and had cost me a lot of money. That visa represented a chance for me to change my life.

After almost two hours I was still waiting, and I was in danger of missing my flight to Milan.

Fortunately, the cheerfulness of the other passengers was contagious, preventing me from losing my good mood.

I had been dreaming of this trip for months; emigrating to Italy had become something of an obsession. At school, at home, on the street, at university, all I talked about was emigrating and landing in this new place where I was going to change my life. When I closed my eyes to go to sleep, I dreamed of opening a clinic and treating people, even those with terminal illnesses; once I had even dreamed of winning a Nobel Prize, and was filled with immense joy.

I liked to let my imagination soar, of course, but I was also a down-to-earth guy and knew how to deal with life's difficulties in a calm way. I had landed at Fiumicino Airport with only my carry-on luggage. In Milan I would collect the large suitcases with only essentials in that I had brought with me.

My flight was in fifty minutes.

I liked my passport photo; the photographer had been good at capturing my best smile and cheerful eyes. It was my first passport; everything had to be perfect. Getting the entry visa had been complicated. I had to pay a fee to have my Science High School diploma translated into Italian, so that it could be recognized as equivalent to an Italian scientific high school diploma. After several long weeks, the official had congratulated me, "*Et voilà, c'est fait! Félicitations!*"

I had spent a lot of money. The immigration process is for a select few; if one has no money, it becomes almost impossible.

After what seemed like an endless wait, with my patience about to run out, a policeman motioned me to approach. My turn had finally come.

I reached the glass box reserved for us non-EU passengers. The passport control officer was having a deep personal conversation with someone on the phone, and was ignoring me. When he finally finished discussing his business, he started flipping through my passport as carefully as he could, scrupulously checking that I was indeed the person in the photograph. He had a wary look on his face, as if he found it difficult to admit that someone of my race might have all their papers in order, and it took him quite a while to hand the document back to me.

14

Mattia, my cellmate, fears nothing. He doesn't believe in chance. He reads a lot. He meditates. He makes his bed every morning. He doesn't cry. But this morning he is sobbing in despair, tears streaming down his face, and before I can ask him what's going on, I hear him exclaim, "Holy shit! This damn prison strips you of everything that makes you feel secure. What a shitty life!"

There had been a suicide. A prisoner hanged himself in the bathroom. His cellmate found him at dawn. When he opened the door early that morning, he found his body hanging from the ceiling, lifeless. Mattia knew the poor man personally, often playing in the yard with him, and I had gotten a glimpse of him a few times in the cafeteria. He was in jail yet again for stealing from a supermarket.

"He was someone I could count on. You know? Just because he was born to a Nigerian father and a mother from Bergamo, he considered himself a citizen of the world. He said he loved life, even though he suffered from severe deprivation and vulnerability in his background. Unfortunately, in the last few weeks we saw each other very little. However, the last time we spoke in the cafeteria, he told me that suicide was a grand exit, a definitive way to erase the sense of one's own inadequacy, living in this world. But I didn't think he would really do it, or I would have done anything to talk him out of it," Mattia tells me, wiping tears from his face with the back of his hand.

"I understand your pain, man," I say, trying to console him. "Unfortunately, he's gone. This was not his place. His bad choices had brought him here, but he did not feel objectively responsible for those choices, and he thought only death could set him free. Friend, life is a gift from Heaven. I tell myself that every morning as soon as I open my eyes."

"Doctor, I've been very unhappy; I've made too many mistakes. But it has never occurred to me to commit suicide. I still have five years to serve in here, but I've decided that when I get out of here, I'll behave differently. The bad luck has to end sometime…"

"What made you change?"

"I have to thank a guy who occupied the bed that is now yours. His name was Nomsa. He taught me to have confidence. He was a person who was full of joy in life… I could barely read or write and everyone made fun of me for it, but he told me I was special and that he would teach me. Which he did. I was lucky to have met him: today I read, I write, I meditate, and I feel free."

"God is just."

"You could say that, doctor. Ever since that man

came into my cell, I seem to have been struck by divine revelation… He also taught me how to pray."

"Do you go to church?"

"No. Nomsa taught me the principles of Buddhism. I don't like the way things work in the Catholic Church."

"Man, I don't like it either. I had a bad experience."

"What happened to you that was so bad?"

"For three months I lived in a hell where I was deprived of freedom, forced to accept absurd rules and submit to them."

"By whom? And what rules are you talking about? Were they drug dealers, gangsters who prey on desperate immigrant workers, mobsters?"

"No. They were so-called decent people: Christians, believers, the leaders of a community that had taken me in when I arrived in Italy."

"Yes, but what did they do to you that was so bad?"

"I'll tell you the surprising truth." With the excuse of talking about my experience, I go back again to when, very young, I set foot in Italy at the beginning of my climb to success.

*

As soon as I landed in Italy, I felt a mixture of happiness and fear. I tried to make myself strong by repeating to myself, "I am successful!" And I felt it strongly in my heart. I was about to start a new life, and nothing could stand in the way of my pursuit of wealth.

I asked myself, "What chance do I have here?" And I

answered, "Here, no one will imprison me in poverty and all the negative thoughts that come with it."

With my head held high, confident that I would be able to fit in immediately, in a flash, I headed for the gate for the domestic flight that in a little over an hour landed at Linate Airport, where an Italian woman was waiting to take me to my new life.

An airport is a world in which you encounter human diversity. Each airport has its own rules, but from the hallways to the stairs and elevators, from the waiting rooms to the security officers and policemen, everything follows a set order.

The terminal is a great junction of people, each pursuing a goal: pilots and stewardesses starting or finishing their shifts, people waiting in line for information or at a café for breakfast or waiting for someone to greet them.

In the midst of those people, for the first time in my life I saw my name written on a placard, being waved by a beautiful hand, long, tapered and white. The woman was young, tall and thin, her dark, fluffy, shiny hair reaching down to her shoulders. She had an oval, pale face with delicate features.

"Hello. Are you Ben?" she asked me in a low, kind voice. She seemed overjoyed to see me.

"Yes, it is I," I confirmed.

"How do you do? My name is Franca. The car is this way. Let's go."

From her gestures, I guessed that fate intended us to be more than just friends.

"Stop looking at her like that," I scolded myself as

we walked out of the airport through the double sliding doors, finding ourselves in the parking lot.

"You'll see; you'll like Italy," she said when we finished loading my things into the trunk of the Fiat Punto. For no reason, she stared at me. Her shining eyes hit me directly in the heart. *My goodness, what a beautiful woman!* I thought as I lowered my gaze, coyly.

"Don't worry; I will personally take care of your Italian," she added.

We left the Milan airport and took the state highway in the direction of Lecco, then took a road that wound through hills, woods and quaint little villages. Franca was driving very slowly, averaging 30 kilometers per hour, careful not to drive us into some ravine.

Suddenly she turned and looked at me, smiling, making my heart race.

I was dying to look into her eyes, but her attention was all on the road, and I was content to examine her discreetly. She was wearing a simple white shirt and a chain with a crucifix around her neck. I looked away. I was nervous as hell. I saw only tenderness in this woman! *Stop it, Ben! This is not a healthy attraction. Remember the promise you made to Sylvie.*

In a few weeks, I would be turning 20. Yes, I was young, but what I needed was not to waste my energy pursuing pleasure. Rather, as I had read in *The Law of Attraction*, if I wanted to accomplish great things in life I needed to learn how to channel my sexual impulse into practical action. Moreover, I was not going to be unfaithful!

We continued up the little road that snaked through

the mountains and stopped in front of a gate that Franca opened with a remote control.

"Here we are; finally we are home!" she exclaimed. We got out of the car. As Franca opened the trunk, I discovered that she had a nice backside. *No, no, no, Ben! You are already busy with Sylvie!*

*

I think back to the last time I had made love with energy, strength and passion with Sylvie, my first girlfriend, in Yaoundé. A beautiful woman. Afterwards, she lay her head on my chest while we were listening to Whitney Houston's *All The Man That I Need*, looking at me with worried eyes, and said, "I know you will forget me."

"No, love, I will write to you every day."

"I don't believe you."

"Why do you say that?"

"Distance kills love!"

"That will not happen to us."

"If you really care about me, why did you decide to leave?"

"Don't ask me that, honey. You know I'm going abroad to study medicine. I love you so much and I promise that then we will never be apart; we will be together for eternity!"

Then we were silent. Without the prospect of eternity, what sense does love have? That had been an honest answer. It was not a lie. But inside I was asking myself, *Is love necessarily monogamous?*

To love is a gift, and I am convinced that love is not a trivial feeling but a firm, strong will to build together with the other person something beautiful and ultimate in life.

I cared for Sylvie very much and we were happy together. She was my first love; it was the first time I devoted myself body and soul to a woman, and I felt that fidelity was a commitment, a promise made to myself. Sylvie and I had been together for five years. She was my age. We went to the same high school in Bafang, but not the same class. The first time I saw her I was enchanted by her shining beauty. At school, during recess, we would gather in small groups, boys with boys and girls with girls, in the corridors and schoolyard, to chat and laugh. Usually among us males we would talk about the beautiful girls in the school, listing them. One of them drove me crazy, and I had decided, if the opportunity arose, to kiss her hand and declare my love for her. That girl was indeed Sylvie. One day I turned around and in the group of girls a few meters away from us I saw her. She hypnotized me. I stood there staring at her for ages; I couldn't tell how long. Finally, she looked up at me and nailed me with a smile. She was talking and laughing. She was moving her delicate hands. She touched her long braids. The features of her chocolate-colored face were as soft as the curves of her body. I was dying to brush up against her, to touch her, to make love to her.

During one of the parties we used to organize in the schoolyard, a sudden burst of joy exploded inside me when I saw she was sitting alone. The two friends who usually kept her company had vacated the chair in front and the one to the side. I jumped at the chance out of fear that someone else would sit down. Finally, we were facing each other.

"Hi, I'm Ben," I introduced myself.

"Hi Ben; I'm Sylvie."

Within seconds I was fantasizing about what I wanted to do with her. The attraction I felt toward her was stirring inside me.

"You're in the first year of the Science High School, aren't you?" she asked me, breaking the ice.

"Yes. And you're in the first year of the Linguistics High School."

She nodded. I was crazy about her. The more we talked, the more a natural mutual understanding developed, as if we were old friends. Had I won her over or was it rather she who had won me over? The important thing was that we liked each other right away. From that time on, we started dating, and I forgot about the other girls I was seeing without commitment.

Alone in my room, I tossed and turned in bed, wondering what kind of alchemy drove a man into the arms of a woman or vice versa, what mystery allowed two beings to remain faithful to each other eternally, even though they were so far apart…

I fell asleep doubting my ability to remain faithful.

In the morning, after showering, I carefully chose what to wear. I dressed mostly in clothes made from African fabric. The choice had been a sensible one, at least since I started going to university in Yaoundé, because all the students tended to buy clothes made in the country in order to support the local economy. After that, it became an established habit. So, for my first day in Don Pietro's community, I wanted to be 100 percent African. I felt tidy and comfortable.

I left my room, took the elevator at the end of the hallway, and went down to the first floor. I was in the large lobby when I saw a beautiful African girl come out who was about my age.

"Hello," she greeted me cordially. "I'm Ernestine, from Rwanda. Nice to meet you, Ben. We were told of your arrival yesterday. May I give you a tour of the house?"

"Gladly. How many people live in this place?"

"Right now, there are about 30 of us – ten Italian volunteers, who are in charge, and 20 Africans. This is a five-star hotel."

"I can see that. A truly luxurious abode. I feel like I'm dreaming!"

"You are mistaken," my guide replied, frowning. "There is little to dream about here."

I said nothing; I did not know what to say. There was an eerie silence. I paused to admire the faux-antique stucco ceiling of the large, empty, dull yellow atrium.

"I bet there's a lot of solidarity in a place like this," I said with a thoughtful air.

"Indeed," the girl confirmed wryly, "a lot of trouble!"

"So why do I sense all this feeling of freedom instead?"

"Only because you don't yet know the laws that govern life here. Soon the landlord you have not yet seen will summon you and talk to you about the contract you have signed or are about to sign. We all have done that. I hope you get used to your new life."

"Don't worry, Ernestine. I'll get used to it. I'm here for a change, for freedom!"

The girl threw me a sidelong glance. "Really?" she replied, bursting out laughing.

I pretended not to notice. There was something ironic and at the same time bitter about Ernestine's words.

We continued to tour the residence as if we were sightseeing. I met other more or less young Africans. From Cameroon: Chantal, Séraphine, Faustin, Henri, André. From Sierra Leone: Mary. From the former Zaïre: Léontine. From Benin: Michel. We asked each other questions about the tribes we belonged to, why we had come to Italy, what we were studying. I proclaimed myself enthusiastic, thinking we were luckier than many other Africans.

"Are you happy here?" I would ask everyone, with a friendly smile.

"Yes, they feed me."

"Yes, they support me in my studies."

"Yes, compared to before I am very well. Thanks to Don Pietro, I can dream of a future education even though I was born in poverty."

All these yeses added up to one certainty: they had the weight of a voluntary choice of submission to the landlord, as if they had passively accepted the condition for their presence there – that they were subservient to Don Pietro's demands. Today it seems clear to me that we were victims of Stockholm syndrome, in which a person who has been kidnapped establishes a bond of affection with his or her captor. Like the slave Stephen in Tarantino's film *Django*

Unchained, the community guests felt satisfied with the annulment of their freedom. And, unfortunately, I was the Django Freeman who appeared and ruined everything, arriving there to break the eggs in the basket…

The bell rang three times to announce lunch. The only one missing at the table was Don Pietro. He did not show up all afternoon, nor did he come to the six o'clock community Mass in the little chapel. In the evening there was a hearty dinner with exclusively Italian food, the same as at breakfast and lunch. I didn't drink coffee because I wasn't used to having it after a meal; then, together with the other Africans, I cleared the table, washed the dishes, glasses and cutlery, cleaned and arranged the dining room and the kitchen. And when I was about to sit in the reading corner of the main lobby to read a newspaper, I was told that Don Pietro wanted to see me in his office.

I walked down the dimly lit hallway. The room, although very tastefully furnished, had a stale air. The priest was reading the Bible, sitting at a marble-topped desk.

"Hello," he greeted me with a smile. "I'm happy to see you. Please have a seat."

Quietly, so as not to betray my feverish excitement, I sat in the high-backed chair in front of him. He kept staring at me, smiling.

"Are you happy to be here?"

"Very," I replied.

"First of all, I want you to know, son, that I am your guide here. Are you ready to follow me?"

"Why are you asking me this?" I asked alarmed.

"There are some points on which I am rather uncompromising, as you will see, because I value your happiness. You come from a poor but Christian family, and I assume that you have great faith in God. This afternoon I had a substitute, but I always personally celebrate Mass in the morning and evening, and I demand to see you from the altar. All I ask of you is exemplary behavior. Agreed?"

I gave a firm nod of agreement.

"Good," he continued. "Do you smoke?"

"No, no!"

"Good. I don't allow smoking in the community. Do you drink?"

"No!"

"Do you listen to African music at full volume?"

"No!"

"Good. Have you ever sinned with a woman?"

"No, no!" I answered, lying. I wondered why he was asking me such an intimate question.

"Wonderful," he said, studying my eyes, perhaps to catch a glimpse of the truth in them. "What do you expect from me?"

"I don't know. I'd like to be of service to the community."

"Perfect. I will be glad to help you achieve the happiness you desire. Are you ready to prove your good faith?"

"I don't know..."

"What? You don't know? Would you sign a document attesting to your loyalty to the community?"

I hesitated.

"Son, it's for your own good! You must trust me; I am here to help you, to make you a capable person."

He stared at me for a moment, then pulled from a cabinet a pre-printed sheet of paper already filled out with my information, and a ballpoint pen. With his finger, he pushed them in front of me.

"Sign here at the bottom, son. I am ready to give you everything you want for your success, but I cannot do so unless you sign these papers first. Please be advised that these are legally binding documents. Please feel free to take a minute to consider before proceeding."

The legal jargon seemed abstruse. Legally binding documents! *Am I about to sign my death warrant? If I report one word of what is written here, how many years would I spend in a place that not even a human rights organization knows the location of?* I asked myself.

But then I convinced myself that I might as well try. So I took the pen, signed and initialed a large number of pages, trembling a little. Inside I knew I had agreed to be manipulated; I just didn't know yet in what way.

"Now," said Don Pietro, "you are part of the community." His smile was different; from being condescending, he now seemed relentless and shrewd, as if I had in fact made… a deal with the devil!

15

I was born in Bafang, a city of about 90,000 people, to a practicing Catholic family. I was baptized one month after birth and had my First Communion and Confirmation together when I was seven years old.

Every Sunday we went to Mass, and in church my parents always sat in the front row. I, forced by my father at the age of eight to become an altar boy, served Mass every Sunday morning. I would wake up to the rooster crowing and wash quickly, and my mother would dress me in my clean 'Sunday clothes'. My whole family and I would leave the house, and together with other believers whom we met on the way, we would reach the parish, which was located at the top of a hill a couple of kilometers from our house.

We walked briskly as the peach-colored sky of dawn gradually gave way to daylight. The only topic of conversation at that time was of miracles and ways to be good Christians. I mostly kept quiet because I didn't care what those indoctrinated adults were saying. While they were talking, I enjoyed brushing my hands over the tall grass and flowers growing on the sides of the road, the same road I used to walk down during the week to go to the Catholic school that was also located at the top of the hill. On Sunday mornings, the bells of St. Mary of Lourdes in Bafang would ring festively to call the faithful together, and the chants sung by the choristers and the faithful resounded in the incense-scented air.

We altar boys would be in rows of two by two behind the crucifer; then there were the seminarians in surplices, and the pastor in mozzetta, surplice and stole. At a nod from the priest, the procession would enter the church and walk down the long aisle between the pews to the altar.

The faithful, mostly women, standing in the rows of pews, would sing with the choir and recite the Our Father and Hail Mary. Our pastor, a white man, would walk tall, at a calm pace, looking left and right, sprinkling holy water through an aspergillum he held in his right hand; as he passed, the faithful would make the sign of the cross, many genuflecting.

The priest was a French missionary, an evangelist of the school of King Leopold II of Belgium, who, in his address given in the year 1883, had requested a lot of tact in evangelization from the 'reverend fathers' and his 'dear countrymen', more in the interest of Belgium than anything else.

The purpose of the mission was not to teach the 'Negroes' the law of God, because they already knew it, but rather to interpret the gospel in a way that would serve the interests of the colonizers in Africa. "We must see to it," Leopold II had said forcefully, "that these savages become disinterested in the wealth they have in abundance underground." It was necessary to use the Gospel so that the faithful Africans would love poverty. 'Blessed are the poor in spirit, for theirs is the kingdom of Heaven. Blessed are the afflicted, for they shall be comforted. Blessed are the meek, for they shall inherit the earth' was the ideal message, just like 'It is easier for a camel to pass through the eye of a needle than for a rich man to enter the kingdom of Heaven'. With the power of persuasion from speeches so close to God's world, the faithful were convinced that there was something extremely risky about freeing oneself to attain a life of riches.

Leopold II's missionaries were expected to infiltrate the social, spiritual and economic organization of the colonized peoples and annihilate every 'mystical and economic system' of the Africans, promoting the Westernization of the younger ones so that as they grew up they would not rebel against the established order. "The children must learn to obey what the missionary recommends to them; he is the father of their souls," the king said in his speech. Then he pointed out, "To evangelize the blacks so that they will remain forever subservient to the white colonialists, so that they will never revolt against the constraints they are under, recite daily 'Blessed are those who mourn, for they will be comforted.'"

Whenever my parents met our pastor, they would genuflect and kiss the ring on the hand the priest extended toward them, then get up and rejoice. I, on the other hand, was reluctant to acknowledge that this man was God's representative on Earth. And indeed, my anger was justified.

How could I not be angry at the one who flogged my parents and my people? While the adults had great respect for the priest, I and a few other kids looked at him with distrust and disgust.

They would force me to stand at the altar with other very young altar boys, who, like me, were new to Sunday service, in order to serve our foreign priest. The faithful, including my parents, would stand in single file in front of the priest; they would turn around, and he would violently hit them in the back with a whip and then shake their hands. The blows resounded throughout the basilica. On seeing this havoc I covered my face with my hand in shame, wondering in bewilderment what terrible crimes those people had been guilty of to deserve such humiliating treatment. But their faces bore enthusiastic and smug expressions, particularly my father's, as if that gesture opened wide for him the gates of Heaven. A sacrifice that would reward him with an extra step closer to the kingdom of Heaven.

This was my parents' life. A life of submission. A life conditioned by *Dum Diversas*, the bull signed on June 16th, 1452 by Pope Nicholas V, born Tommaso Parentucelli. The pontiff recognized the new territorial conquests of King Alfonso V of Portugal; he authorized him to attack, conquer and subjugate the African pagans known as enemies of the faith, to take possession of their goods and lands, to reduce them to perpetual slavery and to transfer their lands and properties to the King of Portugal and his successors.

Many people do not know that before Pope Nicholas V, the Catholic Church had several black, African pontiffs. Pope Victor was elected in 189 and freed a group of Christian prisoners sentenced *ad metalla* – that is, to forced labor – in the mines of Sardinia. Pope Miltiades became pontiff in the year 310, and St. Augustine, his co-religionist, said he was a 'true son of peace… and a true father to Christians'. In 492, when barbarian kings reigned in Rome, Gelasius I was elected Pope. After the Constantinian period, he established a clear distinction between imperial power and the spiritual mission of the Church. He was a very modern and enlightened pope. His writings on the relationship between faith and power set the standard. Dionysius wrote of him, 'He died poor, after having enriched the impoverished.'

To die rich after enriching the poor was my childhood wish, something that I shared only with the rich businessman in our town. My father, on the other hand, wished to die poor in order to deserve the Kingdom of Heaven. Since he could barely support my three sisters, my seven brothers, my mother and me, I had to work hard for my future. When I was seventeen, and until I enrolled in college, a rich businessman employed me as a gardener and servant in his mansion.

In my family, when the subject of money came up, the atmosphere became tense. For my brothers and me, wishing to be rich was forbidden. Money was a taboo subject not only in our house, but in the whole community. If I didn't wake up early enough to pray with my parents, Dad would get sullen and complain in the parish about his sinful son. "He is nothing like I was at his age," he would grumble. If he happened to hear me talk about wealth and money in positive terms, either at home or with friends, he would be overcome with a kind of madness, and punish me. From being the meek man he was, he would be transformed; mercilessly he would whip me with his belt, with a cold and blank expression. The blows could be heard throughout the house.

That punishment seemed really shameful and unjust, yet I always told myself that it was only a bodily punishment, that no one could ever remove my dreams from my head. Although I could not see my father's face when he hit me, and he could not see mine, I think he was ashamed that he was hurting me so badly, but unfortunately that shame turned into fury, prompting him to hit me even harder. Or perhaps I only saw my own shame reflected in his actions. He was acting in that way in the hope of securing Heaven for himself and securing it for me as well… by putting me on the 'straight and narrow'.

Father was born in the village of Bayangam, founded in the 16th century, at the time when in Europe the Treaty of Cateau-Cambrésis defined the accords that ended the Italian wars and the conflict between the Habsburgs and France. Bayangam means 'those who have seen the locusts', because it had suffered a locust invasion.

At first, my father did not know Jesus. When I turned fifteen, I began to ask him questions about why my family was so devoted to the Catholic Church, and especially why they worshiped a white God.

"Who is Jesus?" I asked him point-blank one day.

Father's first reaction was laughter; then he looked up at the sky and replied, "He is salvation, my son. Jesus is salvation."

"Why, Dad?"

"You must know that he saved me from misery, because your grandfather, my father, was a famous sorcerer, a witch doctor who knew the secrets of plants and made remedies from them to cure people. When I turned five, he began to teach me how to recognize plants for every disease. He died when I was only ten years old. And the European missionaries saved me from witchcraft."

"Why witchcraft, Dad?"

"Because my father was a sorcerer, and he was teaching me to become like him."

"So, my grandfather was an evil magician?"

"More or less. He used to teach me bullshit about herbs… about the healing power of his potions. Fortunately, the Church made me realize that this was just nonsense."

"What if it wasn't, Dad?"

In Cameroon, the French colonial administration had given missionaries unfettered power to evangelize, educate and civilize the natives. Orphaned and poor, my father was taken in by Catholic priests who first taught him to fear the God who had European traits. The contents of the books they allowed him to read were combined with images of a white-skinned Jesus, a white-skinned Virgin Mary, and every white-skinned saint. When my father had successfully assimilated Catholic teaching, he became a catechist in his parish; then they allowed him to continue his studies until he graduated as an elementary schoolteacher and was chosen to teach little Europeans.

At that time, the children of European settlers were numerous in the country, attending special schools with programs similar to those in France in order to remain at the same level as their compatriots when the family returned home. European teachers interested in 'international cooperation' (as they put it) were scarce, so my father, a model teacher and practicing Catholic, was chosen as the teacher of the little Europeans in Bafang, the town where I was born. He was the only African teacher in a European school in Cameroon! This privilege was interpreted by him as a miracle of Our Lady of Lourdes, and his faith in the European God grew by leaps and bounds.

Dr. Louis-Paul Aujoulat, a Frenchman born in 1910 in Saïda, Algeria, and a medical graduate from Lille in 1934, had moved to Cameroon, and in 1936 opened a branch of the Ad Lucem Foundation, formed in Lille under the leadership of Monsignor Lienart in Etok.

The French doctor had become a deputy of the People's Republican Movement, a French political party classified as Christian Democrat and centrist; in 1951 he founded his own party, the Cameroonian Democratic Bloc. A few years earlier, in 1947, the Ad Lucem Foundation had established a hospital of the same name in Bafang, and, given the lack of European nursing staff, it had had to recruit and train natives. European missionaries who knew my father's devotion, seriousness and honesty recommended him to the foundation. And so it was that a short time later he found himself in Lille, France, where he stayed for about a year to train as a nursing assistant. Back home, he quickly became a professional nurse, then a medical assistant with his own private practice in the hospital where he could see patients and prescribe medications. In the postcolonial years, he held the position of medical assistant and hospital chief of staff. This success made Our Lady of Lourdes the star of our home, with a corner in the living room dedicated to a large, framed image of her. A crucifix with the white Jesus and numerous statues of Madonnas, from Loreto, Assisi, and Fatima, were all around.

Four of my brothers were enrolled in the small seminary to become priests. They were only supposed to follow the teachings of European missionaries and obey without protest. But my father miscalculated, because we all had our own personalities. We did not like to bow our heads. We were fighting to change our lives, to be the best in society and not in religion or by assimilating into the culture of others. None of my brothers stayed in the seminary for more than a year. After this defeat, my father no longer had the strength to try to push his sons to become servants of God.

16

Andrea is sitting in the interview room. The guard accompanying me leaves us alone and closes the door. My friend gets up and shakes my hand vigorously. After that we sit down and I ask, "Are your investigations going well?"

"Oh, yeah, man. My people are working hard, and we think we know who the real culprit is."

"And who would that be?"

"A 30-year-old man named Giacomo Suardi. Do you remember the black Ford Fiesta that tailed you?"

*

Yes. I remember it.

One Friday, a little after seven thirty, I was behind the wheel of my Audi and was pulling out of the hospital parking lot when I looked in the side mirror and noticed that a black Ford Fiesta was on the road about ten meters behind me.

I had to stop at Princi's Bakery to pick up Kemi's birthday cake, which my wife had ordered. There was only one girl waiting, and Maria, the baker, was busying herself behind the counter.

"Hello, Maria."

"Hi, Doctor, how are you doing?"

"Fine. How about you? Your menopause?"

"It's getting worse, Doctor; the hot flushes won't leave me alone! Especially at night. Going through menopause at only 45 is hell. It's bad, Doctor; do you know I can't make love to my husband anymore? It's all dry down there; it hurts and sometimes it bleeds when he pene—"

"I understand, Maria. Come by and see me at the hospital when you can, and we'll see what to do. Umm, my wife ordered a cake under my name this morning."

Maria entered the small room behind her and came out with a cardboard cake box. "Here it is." She handed me the cake and I paid.

"Thank you, Maria."

"Thank you, Doctor. I'll come to your office tomorrow."

"I'll be waiting for you. Come any time," I concluded as I left the bakery.

As I opened the door of my car, which was double-parked, my gaze fell on the black Ford Fiesta parked nearby, ten meters behind my Audi. That car looked exactly like the one I had noticed when I was leaving the hospital parking lot.

I stopped several times at traffic lights, and the car was always behind me. I zig-zagged down many streets and stopped at yet another traffic light. Looking in the rearview mirror, I could see that the third car back was the black Ford. It was evidently tailing me.

*

"Well, the owner of that car is Giacomo Suardi, originally from Caserta... All this information was given to me by Sarah."

"Who is Sarah?"

"Sarah is my best assistant – young, and determined to prove your innocence and get you out of here as soon as possible. She thinks the killer might be that Casertan guy."

"Really?"

"Really."

"Thank you, man. But how were you able to identify that car? I don't remember ever giving you the license plate number, and so I don't..."

"Indeed. Here's what happened. Sarah was investigating Mr. Monti. She had parked her car in a driveway and was listening to music at a very low volume, surveying the building that he lived in; then, after waiting an hour, the man came out. She saw him walking along the sidewalk, and she got out of the car to follow him, giving him a head start of at least a hundred meters. It was ten o'clock at night and the street was deserted. She did not want Monti to hear her footsteps.

"Suddenly he stopped and opened a car door. Sarah saw it was a black Ford Fiesta. There was someone behind the wheel waiting for him; they started the car and sped off as soon as he got in."

"Then what happened?"

"Unable to run back to get her Fiat Punto to chase the Ford, Sarah pulled her cell phone out of her pocket and took some pictures of the car as it was driving away. She is very stubborn. She hates leaving a job unfinished once she has started."

Without a doubt, she was the perfect partner for Andrea, who has solved many murder cases in his 20 years of lawyering. Although he does not like to brag, his colleagues consider him a winner.

"I still don't understand how you came to connect Giacomo Suardi to all this."

"Simple. Based on the license plate photo, we checked out the number and learned that Suardi registered the Ford Fiesta a year ago. At least that's what they say here."

Andrea hands me documentation issued by the Milan DMV.

"We made inquiries into the man's background and obtained his criminal record from the court in Milan. Eighteen years ago he was involved in an assassination attempt against a left-wing politician, who fortunately survived. He was only sentenced to one year because, although he was part of the group of terrorists who planned and executed the ambush, he – Suardi – was not directly responsible… Later, he was sentenced to two years and three months for robbery, and again, after a very difficult trial, the Supreme Court found him guilty in the death of a young and attractive married woman – involuntary manslaughter. He was given a reduced sentence; no one knows why."

"What is the connection between him and Monti?"

"They are in the same political group. On the party payroll, he is listed as a driver and bodyguard. Bank documents show that in recent months, Monti has made significant payments to him, up to 30,000 euros."

"For what purpose?"

"That's what I would like to find out. Maybe to kill you."

"I am alive! Barbara was killed. If he was given that money to kill me, then why didn't he do it?"

"I don't know…"

"Why did he kill that poor woman?"

"I don't know, Ben. He must have thought that she was your lover and that you loved her so much you would grieve over her death."

"To me this murder makes no sense."

"No, it makes sense. Let's stick close to these racists' asses, take pictures of whatever they do when they meet. Let's keep our eyes open and find out how those two set you up."

"Thank you, man. Seriously, thank you! This is great news! I've been locked up here for two weeks. My wife came to see me yesterday. She can hardly believe that your investigation is making any progress. But when she calls me tomorrow, I will tell her that we are close to finding the killer."

Andrea gives me a reassuring smile.

"It's okay, Ben. Don't worry; I'll get back to you with good news."

17

I jolt awake from a bizarre dream. I was in a battlefield in A.D. 300, and my fellow soldiers and I were attacking a fortification. Soldiers on horseback and on foot were fighting; however, instead of ancient armor, the soldiers wore contemporary uniforms, similar to those of marines. The combatants were Africans and Europeans. Leading the army that was gaining the upper hand was an African horseman on a black horse. He was fighting with determination, confronting his enemies and striking them from side to side with his sword. There was blood everywhere! The defeated fell like dead branches, some of them running away. They looked like wild animals. They screamed in despair as their commander and other soldiers surrendered, kneeling before the African general, majestically seated on his black horse.

I am drenched in sweat and trying to calm down. Who was that victorious general? Perhaps it was Saint Maurice. He was the general of the Roman Empire at the head of the legendary Theban legion in Mesopotamia, transferred to Roman Central Europe, Cologne and the northern Alps. He is the patron saint of the Alpine Corps and the Swiss Guards. In 926, the sword of St. Maurice was part of the imperial throne property of Henry I; it was used until 1916 for the coronation of Austro-Hungarian emperors. In the cathedral in Magdeburg, Germany, images of St. Maurice depict him with dark skin and distinctly African features. I wonder if the protagonist from my dream was really he, St. Maurice.

Mattia is asleep with his mouth wide open, snoring, sounding like an electric saw. I sit on the bed and stretch. Before getting up to go to the bathroom, I close my eyes and try to meditate, but my mind takes me to the last tense conversation I had with my father a week before I left Cameroon for Italy.

*

"Do you want to humiliate me? Do you want to dishonor your family?"

"What's the problem, Dad?" I asked sharply, without looking him in the eye. I knew how much he suffered from the choices I made.

He resented the fact that it was another person, richer than he, who was financing my trip.

"You're just telling me out of the blue that you want to move to Europe?"

"I'm so sorry, Dad, but I also told you two weeks ago."

"Huh?"

We were at the table, having breakfast. I began to scratch my right eyebrow, my lower lip protruding slightly. Dad found that expression exasperating.

"Why are you making that face?"

"What face, Dad?"

"You look disgusted with me," he blurted out.

"I don't feel that way, Dad."

"Yes, you do!"

I avoided his gaze and did not respond. That passive attitude sent him into a rage.

"You really want to bring shame to this family, huh?"

"No, Dad. That's not my intention."

"You shouldn't have gone around asking for money!"

"Excuse me, Dad, but I would like to become a doctor," I said in a near whisper. I also wanted to add, *"I just want to change my life, make it better, so I'm leaving,"* but he beat me to it.

"I will not accept such dishonor from my son!"

My father and I had come to this conflict after almost a year of me studying at the university in Yaoundé, far from home.

After graduating from high school, with the money I had earned and saved working for the wealthy businessman, I had managed to realize my ambition to pursue my studies at the university.

On weekends during school time, and almost every morning at seven o'clock, I had gone to work at the mansion of that wealthy businessman. It was not only the daily pay that interested me, but also the affluent life that family had. For two years, until I came of age, I had gone there very happily and with determination. There I realized day by day that I was experiencing the best days of my life, not least of all because I was joyfully and effortlessly tending the lawn and its wonderful flowers; because my employer's wife almost always brought me water or juice to drink; and because then at lunchtime she would delight me with delicious dishes that I ate inside the house. I felt like I had landed in a new world of luxury, elegance, and the many books displayed in the library corner of the living room.

The lady noticed my burning desire to devour those texts and allowed me to read them, filling me with great curiosity and happiness. All those books were there at my disposal; I just had to find the time to read them! So, I asked the lady's permission to stay in the mansion after I finished work at three in the afternoon. Aware of my thirst for knowledge, she allowed me to stay every day for about a year, from three o'clock until six in the evening, reading books, a habit that could bring me much peace.

I was particularly attracted to books about individual wealth; those volumes spoke to me as no textbook had done before. To absorb the teachings that would really change my life, I would take refuge in the back garden, near the garage that contained the owner of the mansion's three luxury cars. I would sit on a bench under a tree with book in hand, and, like a Buddhist in meditation, focus on the pages that one after another guided me to my current pattern of life.

At some point I literally moved to another dimension, totally overwhelmed by a feeling of love. I had understood very clearly why I was living in poverty, why above all I did not have to continue with that kind of thinking marked by deprivation, of what role each person in my family played, and in general how life worked. I recognized that I had acquired a very healthy energy. I had just discovered the meaning of 'I am'. In those words, Jesus tells us that he is one with God: 'I am the resurrection, and the life: he that believeth in me, though he were dead, yet shall he live' (John 11:25). Jesus means that God is the resurrection, the eternal being of light that resides in each of us. The two words 'I am' are the name of God. In the book of Exodus, God says to Moses, "I am who I am." I don't think I am committing the sin of blasphemy by suggesting that God lives in me: *I am God*, because *I am*. But the concept that anything is possible must be firmly rooted in the depths of our imagination: the more I believe in my personal divine nature, the more it begins to become real to me.

One day, informed by his wife of my passion for reading, the wealthy businessman had joined me in the garden, and to encourage me, said, with his usual simplicity and humility in his dealings with people, "I hear you are a great reader! That's wonderful!" In time he moved on to giving me reading recommendations, and I soon discovered that I enjoyed the same books he did, the ones on personal growth. Once I had gained a degree of confidence that allowed me to speak frankly, he started to show me the way to dream big and the secret to becoming as rich as he was, a path carved out mostly through determination and perseverance. The more I read, the more I realized that I was happy. In that man's world, fear of poverty was not contemplated; there was no talk of fighting poverty, but only of how to attract abundance to oneself, how to achieve financial success in any endeavor and the willpower needed to get there, making the impossible possible. That happy discovery would gradually undo the harmful principles that had been inculcated in me from childhood, so that I would focus only on failure and misery. I no longer had a tremendous fear of poverty. That destructive anguish was no longer conditioning my mind, and I was able to plan a future full of wealth and abundance. I was at the peak of happiness, imbued with a feeling of love, inner peace, and health.

The rich businessman gave me some good advice: "Successful people give the best of their abilities in everything they undertake and do. You must always work as if one of your superiors is watching you every minute of every day!" Thus, I learned that whatever I did, I always had to give my best. Knowing how to overcome life's many failures was the key to success for him. "You have to have a vision for your life; it doesn't matter where you start, but where you end up," he said.

Some time later, with the money I had earned, I finally moved to Yaoundé, the capital, where the country's only university was. I was there to take the medical school admission test. In front of the bulletin board displaying the results were about five or so students looking for their names. I felt confident, serene. I hurriedly scanned the list of those admitted. I could not find my name.

I calmly reread every name of the sixty admitted students, sure that I was wrong. Nothing. My name was not there. A punch in the gut. Nothing has quite such a devastating effect on a student who has always been at the top of the class than a sudden rejection. Still, I closed my eyes and forced myself to stay calm.

"I definitely missed something," I said to myself, taking a deep breath, then opened my eyes again. I rested the tip of my index finger under the line of each name to make sure I didn't miss mine. Zilch. *Rien*. Nothing. Denied. What a disappointment.

"Do you realize... what fools we are?" said one student, who had also been rejected.

"But I'm sure I answered all the questions correctly," I replied, firmly.

"Oh yeah?"

"Yes!"

In my Science High School graduation, I had gotten the highest grade. And I had studied hard for that test. To tell you the truth, I knew it was very difficult to get in, and that's exactly why I had immediately thrown myself headlong into studying.

"Friend, unfortunately we know how things go in this country; if you are not the son of a big shot, all the doors will be closed to you. This test is like the one you take to get hired at NASA; every year there are more than 2,000 applicants for about 70 positions, and it is well known that more than two-thirds of those selected are ones who bribed the committee," said another failed candidate.

"But it's not fair!" I replied.

"Cre-ti-n," said the legion of rejects in unison, mocking me.

"Medicine is my number one aspiration," I said on

the phone to Célestin after informing him that I had not been admitted. He was my childhood friend. We had met in school, but he dropped out in fifth grade; sometimes I envied him when I saw the life he was leading.

"Come work with me! I need someone who is educated like you to manage the staff. Would you like to?"

Célestin was almost an *illettré*, an illiterate; he could barely read and write, but he was very intelligent. After his failure in school, he had done what many did, indeed, what most of the population did, since the state did not like knowledgeable brains: he had given up on his studies and thrown himself into *débrouillardise*, that is, the art of making do. It was like that in my country: the more educated you were, the more of a threat you posed to the regime imposed by France. My friend had started out first as a *laveur de voitures* (car-washer) on the street, then got into the business of buying and selling goods from the West, and thus became a wealthy trader with stores in Bafang, Yaoundé, and several other cities. At only nineteen years of age! He loved women, even though he was married, and had a three-month-old son. He owned a large mansion and a Mercedes, and this luxury appealed to the girls. I must admit that sometimes he helped me with money.

"No. I told you I have been rejected, not that I want to drop out of school. Do you understand me?"

"Yes, I understand you. But I can't help you. What do you intend to do now?"

"Since I am not in a position to change things, I am forced to fall back on natural science."

I admit it: I was no longer studying with the same enthusiasm; I was no longer reading. I was missing the passion. I had always dreamed of getting a medical degree, of being useful to society by treating people.

Nevertheless, I kept hoping that fate would allow me to hit my goal.

I had been going to university for only two months, bored out of my mind. The fact that I was seeing a lot of Sylvie, who, after high school, had enrolled in modern literature in Yaoundé, did not change anything. Sometimes depression, like a vampire, sucked my blood and left my heart dry. But I did not throw in the towel because I was convinced that something important would happen sooner or later. Yes, at that moment, my life was flat; I had the impression that I was sailing by sight but that what was going to happen would be decisive and essential for me. I could feel it. I like to fantasize, to travel with my mind. I've been doing it for as long as I can remember.

*

Many years ago, when I was a teenager, my father punished me. Because I liked girls, I had kissed one of my classmates at a parish party. A spontaneous, innocent kiss. I was still a virgin at the time. But when the parish priest told my father what I had done, he, indoctrinated by the Catholic Church regarding carnal sin, didn't even give me time to explain or apologize. He gave me two slaps and then locked me in the punishment room, where I was isolated whenever I broke Church rules.

My mom used to bring me food there. She was beautiful, sweet and good. She knew that I would never change my hostile attitude toward my father's dogmatic faith and that I would never become a religious fanatic, because freedom of thought was too important to me. When she brought me food we would talk, and she would always try to convince me that what my father was doing was for my own good, for my future. She would ask me to change. She was trying to scare me with the fear that God's wrath would come down on me and make me crazy if I continued to disobey.

I got used to the darkness of that room. I thought there was no point in being defined through someone else's need. I did not want to be regarded as a baby in this harsh land that never conceded anything without exacting a price. I harbored within me the desire not to follow in my parents' footsteps, not to resemble them, and the hot blood coursing through my veins made me more than ever a child of the modern world.

How could my parents impose the rules of the colonial past on me? Europeans had lost their colonies in Africa but continued to crush Africans' right to freedom with neocolonialism. The horrible thing about modern racism devised by the West in the post-colonial era is not religion, but the certainty that Africans cannot reach God and salvation without the help of white Europeans, together with the enormous presumption that they belong to a superior race. My generation has television; people move easily from one country to another; and there are various movements to fight for human rights. I could not understand why my parents did not see that the very doctrine they were trying to impose on me taught me about inequality amongst men. From the moment I was born, I had heard that the 'black race' was inherently inferior to the 'white race'; and Western religions wanted to shame us for being Africans so that, as we became adults, we would joyfully renounce being who we are.

Yes, I lived for years and years in the ritual of praying the *Hail Mary Mother of God* prayer... and the *Our Father who art in Heaven* prayer... We recited the litany of divine mercy and the poor, in the morning at six o'clock before breakfast, at lunch and at dinner, every day. My parents were striving to make us true Christians, they said. They would have preferred me and my older brothers to all become priests, and my two younger sisters, nuns. This obsession could only be explained by the fact that in Cameroon, immediately after the onset of the post-colonial period, the privileges of a Western life were more readily granted to new local priests and 'indigenous officials', as they were called by the post-colonial administration. Therefore, fortune kissed every family that managed to have a priest or nun for a son or daughter.

My father used to talk to us all the time about Heaven, and he only felt good when he knelt in church at the foot of the porcelain statue of the European Madonna. For him, talking about money was taboo, just like sex; he always praised the virtue of poverty only. That's why I didn't have the courage to demand financial support after my high school graduation.

Natural science classes bored me to tears. I felt

my future was at stake. What was the point of having a degree just to have it? I didn't like the idea of pursuing a profession without passion; I wanted to be a doctor, nothing else. I wandered the streets trying to devise a way to achieve my dream. Passing through bare and dilapidated neighborhoods inhabited by miserable people, the rejection of poverty grew in me. I took classes at the university out of a sense of duty, but with my mind elsewhere, so I took notes summarily, often making mistakes. Deep down I knew there was a way out of that prison. I used to laugh it off, but slowly, a goal was forming in me: to study at a major medical school in the West and become a famous surgeon.

I knew that this desire would be achieved. In life, desire counts first; the more you wholeheartedly desire something, the more it becomes possible to obtain and achieve it. By focusing your mind on what you desire, you can almost make it real.

Every night I went back to my small room in the university dorms. It was cheap and uncomfortable, but it was close to the campus and the cafeteria. The only furniture I had consisted of a bed with a broken mattress, a table that doubled as a desk, and a chair.

When I was feeling very dejected, I would wander around the neighborhood, go into a bookstore, or sit outside a café with a beer in my hand and watch sadly as people passed by on the sidewalk. The bartender would occasionally come out and look at me to let me know that I had to order something more so that I could sit there. I was sweating from the heat, but instead of staying cool inside the café I was sitting outside, my mind slowly drifting away until I could no longer hear the chaotic noises around me. I saw myself as a well-off man.

I wished to be rich one day. What was wrong with me? Why couldn't I have some of those beautiful things I saw every day on TV and in the newspapers, the things Europeans enjoyed?

Late one afternoon, as I was returning to the university dorms, I found a book on the ground. I stopped and picked it up. It was entitled, *The Law of Attraction*. I leafed through it and knew immediately that it was something interesting. One passage in particular struck me: 'All people, circumstances, situations and events are drawn toward you by the power of the thoughts you produce.'

I decided to take it home. It was one of those chance discoveries that changes your view of the world. Every night before I went to sleep, I read a few pages of it, and I began to think about my life in a new way, the way I wanted it to be.

Throughout the day I would keep asking myself, "What do I want in life?" The only answer was that I wanted to become a doctor; and immediately I felt better.

One Sunday, after several months, I entered the church. Since I had left the home of my parents, who forced us, as children, to attend church, it was not natural for me to go there. Mass was being celebrated by a sad old European missionary; he was shabby, had a hunchback and moved awkwardly. He introduced himself as Don Pietro. I felt very sorry for him.

I felt lost, and I was looking for support from someone,

perhaps rich and generous, who could help me achieve my goals. And that 'poor guy' who had introduced himself at the beginning of his homily as Don Pietro didn't seem like the right person for me because he seemed clueless.

After Mass I decided to go and say hello to Sister Andreina, who had moved two years earlier to the parish in Yaoundé, to the orphanage adjacent to the church. Like Don Pietro, she was Italian. I had met her in Bafang: she ran an orphanage there as well. She was very close friends with my parents. When she came to our house for dinner, she always asked me to give her a hand at the orphanage, and I gladly lent myself to washing floors, mowing the lawn, taking the children for walks, helping them with their homework.

I met Sister Andreina in her office. She left the packages she was arranging in a corner of the room, and welcomed me with a warm, sisterly hug.

"So good to see you again, Ben!"

"You too, Sister."

"You know, these packages are gifts sent by some Italian benefactors who have adopted my children from a distance. What are you doing around here?" she asked, pointing to one of the two chairs next to the desk as she sat on the other.

"I go to the university. I should have stopped by to say hello when I arrived in Yaoundé six months ago!"

"That's okay. How's school going? You're in medicine, right?"

"No. I didn't get in, and enrolled in natural science..."

"I'm sorry. I know how much you wanted to be a doctor. That's all you talked about in Bafang."

"Sister, I am sure I will realize my dream, although I don't yet know how."

"Son, the ways of the Lord are infinite!"

I gasped. Those words did not come from the nun, but from the voice of a male behind me.

"Don't you know who I am, son? I am the founder of this community, and I help so many poor kids like you!" said the man.

His patronizing attitude paralyzed me. This man whom I had believed to be clueless was in fact not. I was silent; I could not speak.

The man looked at me for a few moments, then introduced himself: "My name is Don Pietro, son."

"And I'm Ben…"

In a few words the nun explained to the priest who I was and that she valued me because I had gone out of my way for their community in the past. Then she apologized and left us alone.

"You are the first African to speak so determinedly about wanting to achieve his dream."

"The first?"

"Yes, in this poor part of the world, people act without thinking about the future; they prefer to reap immediate benefits, even if they do not bring happiness. An African is like a child; just treat them with a little common sense and give them something to live for, and you get everything you want from them. The African dreams, but—"

"They don't look farther than the tip of their own noses?"

"That's right."

"That's not my case, Father. I would be really useful to society if I studied medicine."

"I can help you by welcoming you into my large community in Valsassina. For now, however, there is no money to pay for your ticket and travel. Who knows? Maybe I can find a benefactor the next time I come to Cameroon."

I wanted to stand and jump for joy – finally! – but I restrained myself and remained seated and silent. A minute of silence. Then I asked, "When do you plan to return, Father?"

"Next year, always around this time."

"No, no, no, Father! I can't wait so long. I want to go now!"

"If you pay for your trip, I will take care of you in Italy. The door of my community is already open for you. Come whenever you want."

"I'll find the money, Father!"

"Good. Good luck, son!"

I said those words having in mind the rich businessman, the only person who could help me find the money. He had paid for my tuition at the University of Yaoundé and promised to help me out.

"My son, how much does this ambition of yours cost?" said the businessman, when we next spoke.

"Just the plane ticket, and maybe, if possible, some money to survive a few months in Italy."

"In Italy? I was thinking in France!"

"Yes, in Italy. I met with Don Pietro, an Italian priest who will put me up in his community."

"How did you meet him?"

"Through a nun who knows my family."

"Ah! But… you don't speak Italian!"

"I will learn it when I get there, on the spot. The nun has volunteered to give me a crash course in conversation before my departure."

"Boy, don't you think you're getting ahead of yourself?"

"No, I feel this is the right thing to do. In life, dreams matter. I still have three months until the entrance test for medical school in Milan."

"If you say so! You have my blessing and support."

Right after that conversation with the rich businessman, I had to inform my biological father. Therefore, the next day I found myself with my family in Bafang, having lunch with him alone.

"My son, recite the prayer with me."

We bowed our heads.

"Lord, thank You for Your goodness in this world. Thank You for the intelligence You have given my son. Bless him always, please, and fulfill his wishes. Amen."

We raised our heads.

"Thank you, Dad, for the esteem you've always had for me."

My mother, a plus-sized woman intent on tidying up the house, never still, always quick to find something to do, came in with a piping hot dish. Dad and I found ourselves alone with our plates full of food.

Sitting in front of my father, I announced, mid-sentence: "Dad, I am about to leave our country."

He froze with his spoon full of beans in mid-air and looked me in the eye.

"What does that mean?"

"That I want to leave. To go abroad!"

"Abroad?"

I nodded.

"Why?"

"To become a doctor. It's my dream – you know."

"Yes, I know, but are you crazy? How did you come up with this idea? Where are you going to get the money?"

"Money is not a problem, Dad. I already have it!"

"Ah! And where did you get it?"

"I have a benefactor."

Silence. Nothing could be heard except a soft noise, and it wasn't my mother sorting things out in the kitchen, or Amie, our dog, waiting under the table for a few bites. It was Dad's spoon as he furiously picked up the food, tapping on the plate, trembling. That puzzling silence lasted almost ten minutes. Then he broke it.

"I cannot accept such humiliation from you."

18

We can go out into the fresh air accompanied by prison officers. When I go out mid-afternoon, following my usual after-dinner reading, my eyes struggle to adjust, going from the dimness to the blinding light. Then I remember where I am: in the San Vittore prison in downtown Milan. There are two basketball hoops in the small courtyard, and on the walls are some murals painted by inmates. The heat is stifling, and you can hear the sounds of traffic.

One day, Mattia said, "I think the sounds coming from the street, the horns, traffic noise and people's voices, are good for us inmates. Inside the thick walls of the prison, you can't hear anything, but when you go outside, you can. The beauty of San Vittore is that it is in the city; the other Milanese prisons are in the open countryside, and there is a lot of silence. So being here, the outside world is not a distant memory for us. Some people come outside just to breathe in a little of the life they had before, and won't have for a while."

I am actually not in the courtyard to get some air, but because Mattia invited me here to get acquainted with his friends – Mahmoud, Samuele, Ivan, Fabrizio, Ousmane, Johnny, and also Diouf, whom I have not heard from since we clashed in the cafeteria. We stand in a circle near a wall covered in murals, and we talk.

"Good morning. My name is Ousmane Tarib. I was the imam of a large Muslim community in Milan. It has been exactly one year since I was locked up here because I was falsely accused of terrorism, of indoctrinating and recruiting young people from the mosque for the war in Syria. That is false."

I am intrigued by this short man in his 60s, hunched over, which makes him look even more petite, but with an austere demeanor, especially when he speaks. He has a deep, booming voice. Mattia told me about him last night, but, inviting me to join this group that he described as being 'for moral support and sharing', he did not tell me that the imam who founded it six months ago is a terrorist.

"Mahmoud Asfa; nice to meet you, Ben. Does my name ring a bell?"

"Should it?"

"Yes, it should."

"Tell me again, please?"

"Mahmoud Asfa."

"Oh! Were you my friend during my freshman year at college? We played on the same basketball team. I have good memories of a sensitive guy from a good Egyptian family, always ready to be supportive, who made friends with everyone."

"That's right."

"Of course, with the full beard you have now, I would never have recognized you. Excuse me, but I didn't think I would meet you in prison. What did you end up in here for?"

"For burning a cross and being a member of a fundamentalist movement markedly hostile to the West."

Asfa was born in Italy and was granted Italian citizenship at the age of 19. He had invited me for feast twice: first to his home for dinner with his parents and his slightly older sister; and then to a restaurant, when we won the inter-university championship, and his mother had given me a traditional outfit from Egypt. I still remember, especially at the first dinner, the particularly fraternal welcome and the abundance of Arabic food. That family had given me access to a new culture and faith, broadening my mind and heart to realize that meeting sincere people contributes to our well-being and that of mankind. Those are not gestures that go unnoticed. We need to not feel lonely, and how can you not welcome with your heart a boy, a girl, a man, a woman, a family that needs affection more than food and a home?

"My name is Ivan Jankovic, and I'm here because I killed my—"

A fierce scream from across the courtyard chills everyone's blood.

"What is that?"

We see blood spurting from the nose of the inmate who shrieked. He had brought his hands in front of his face but was unable to avoid the slap delivered by the thug with the tattooed neck, which was hard enough to make him stagger. The tattooed man approaches and delivers another, even harder.

"Don't ever fuck with me again!" screams the behemoth.

The unfortunate man covers his head with his arms, but the third blow is a punch in the stomach that sends him falling to the ground. The tattooed man takes the opportunity to pounce on him.

"No one, no one, no one is going to fuck with me, understand?"

The battered inmate rolls over, trying to catch his breath.

*

We are prisoners here, but like every human being, we long for freedom.

I had always particularly desired it, freedom, even in Cameroon, amidst the toil of people earning a living. Then I claimed it within the walls of Don Pietro's community. At that time, I was 19 years old and there was a whole world out there to discover. I did not understand why I had to stay in that community. I felt disconnected; I harbored a lot of anger; but I knew I had to do something.

We Africans in the community were stuck there all the time doing all kinds of jobs. We used to wash dishes during weekends when they were training aspiring volunteers for Africa. Those conferences were devoted to figuring out the best ways to make the continent permanently dependent on charity organizations. Yes, every week, hundreds of clients arrived at this large hotel disguised as a 'Christian community'. In the chain of production, we Africans were presented as fulfilling duties as pious subjects, but in fact we were maintenance workers. The house was always clean, and Don Pietro's affairs blossomed. We attended Masses, prayed and attended follow-up meetings, often trembling for fear of being reprimanded for making a mistake. We had no salaries, no contracts, no social security contributions, no rights.

We had the appearance of robots.

We would have dinner at 7.30, and when I was late to the mess hall, a frightened 'brother' would whisper in my ear, "You can't go on like this, Ben, I'm telling you for your own good. You are always late for everything. Do you know that the Don can send you back down to Africa?"

At 10.30, after night prayer, there was a curfew. Sometimes, at that hour, I liked to sit in the TV room, but I would no sooner turn on the television than some higher-up in the community would pop in and turn it off, ordering me to go to sleep.

The anger inside me was growing more and more blinding. I clenched my fists in order to contain it. I was afraid that one day the blood would rush to my head, and I would snap and become violent. Perhaps to some extent they wanted that to happen.

I remember when I smoked my first cigarette with some classmates, when I was fifteen years old. We were in a school hallway during recess, clustered in a corner, and we passed the cigarette from one to another. I never smoked again, but that day I felt animated by the typical youthful conformity that drives one to imitate adults in order to be accepted by the group. I never even tried drugs like so many of my peers.

Anyway, at one point, there was a collective stampede and they all ran away. I turned my head and saw the principal's inquisitive gaze aimed at me. The last of the gang to disappear had slipped his cigarette between my fingers. Without a word, the principal took it out of my hand and crushed it on the ground. I kept quiet. Then I got a good scolding, and due to teenage arrogance, I told the principal to go to Hell. In the afternoon, the disciplinary board was convened and unanimously voted to suspend me for two weeks. Fortunately, I was very young, and this did not in fact affect my future.

In Don Pietro's community, on the other hand, the slightest mistake would have jeopardized my aspirations. I was aware that standing up to the founder of the community, a person feared by everyone in there, and a person with great economic power – a power that had very little to do with Christianity – would have been the equivalent of throwing away my beautiful hopes.

But I was seething with anger and would not be able to contain myself forever; I could feel it. I was no longer the person I had been at the beginning of that experience, when I was dispensing consolation and kindness to everyone. I, too, had begun to complain and was no longer mindlessly doing everything they wanted me to do. Hearing Don Pietro call us 'son!' or 'daughter!' with the deep conviction that he rightfully owned us was beginning to seriously bother me.

I had become grumpy, frustrated. I suffered Don Pietro's authority as a personal wrong, a low blow to my expectations. I felt trapped, at a dead end. What was I supposed to do?

To let off steam, during afternoon Mass, I would go running in the beautiful garden full of flowers and plants. I did not listen to the rumors about me that were going around in the community because I was too engrossed in my inner turmoil and was constantly brooding, building a fire under the ashes.

While some of my classmates were forcibly kept down by Don Pietro, the rest were willingly submissive; they really believed, in some way, in their own inferiority – a kind of brainwashing that I did not feel I could accept for much longer. I would write to Sylvie, talking to her about the plans for our future, telling her that I loved her very much and that without her I felt lost. And it was true: only the thought of our love kept me going.

I, who considered myself a quiet guy, was now always furious.

I spent more than an hour drafting a sorrowful letter to Don Pietro, a thoughtful letter in which I explained my concerns for my freedom. I complained about everything, begged him to find me accommodation in Milan immediately. But once I had signed, reread, folded it and stuffed it in an envelope, I was struck by doubts of conscience. I had a great desire to escape from that seclusion, but a very sweet voice whispered to me that I was making a grave mistake. Another voice, cold and determined, commanded me to go immediately and deliver the letter to him.

"That priest is against your happiness!" it thundered. Unfortunately, I listened to the first voice, the one that seemed like the voice of wisdom. My hands shaking, I stared at the envelope with infinite sadness, reopened it and angrily tore it up for fear of making an irreparable mistake!

•

19

At the end of the long hallway, the officer who escorted me opens the door to the interview room.

I go immediately to the table where Roger is waiting for me. He gets up to come and hug me but the officer guarding me forbids him to do so, and we are limited to a handshake – which, however, is firm and warm. I make my way to the table, following him. Taking a seat, I observe Roger, now in front of me. He has shaved off his gray hair and looks fitter than ever; the heart attack he had a year ago has almost rejuvenated him. He has lost weight.

I still remember that evening at Malpensa. I was there to greet him after a month-long business trip to Africa. At 8pm on the dot, Roger went through the sliding glass doors of the arrivals hall and immediately dropped to the ground. The other passengers were frightened, while I, being a doctor, understood what was happening and rushed to my friend's aid.

"I do believe in your innocence. Even journalist Marco

Ghini, who had defended you in *Corriere della Sera*, is giving the media a misleading picture of you," Roger says, looking me straight in the eye as he crosses his arms over his belly. "He claims he misjudged you because you look different from other Africans. There is a prevailing racism in the newspapers and on television. Do you remember when we were younger and committed to our future?"

"How could I forget, Roger?"

Roger and I met as students; we shared a two-bedroom dorm in the university dormitory on Via Bassini in Milan. At the time we were young college students far from our families, and full of dreams. The friend I knew was a rather self-centered guy. He needed to draw attention to himself and always dressed up to impress girls. He spent his university grant money on having fun: women, clubs and luxury things. Fortunately, he did not get drunk, take drugs or gamble.

At the university and in daily life, underhand acts of racism made us realize that we Africans were considered inferior. One evening, after a tiring day of studying, we had stayed up late talking about racial capitalism, and in the end we had concluded that we had to study like crazy and aim very high if we wanted to become rich and free ourselves from prejudice.

So we both graduated with highest grades and *cum laude*. As an engineer out of Politecnico di Milano, Roger always delivered to his superiors a job well done and on time; and ten years ago he was appointed director for Africa by the same Italian oil company that had granted him the scholarship to immigrate to Italy. He was hard-working, tireless, and so top management promoted him. During his business trips he traveled first class, both by train and plane, slept in luxurious suites in five-star hotels, and had high-end cars with chauffeurs in tow in every city. All expenses were paid by the company, which, in addition, gave him a bonus for each overseas mission. He enjoyed the privileges for which he had long hoped and yearned.

"Ben, we fought to become important professionals in this country. Everything we have, we have earned. Know that I'm here to help you, man!"

"Thank you. I know I can count on you."

A few months earlier, I had asked him for a favor. After the surgery on Mrs. Angela Rossi, I was locked in my office. I made myself a coffee with the machine my wife had given me, took off my lab coat and picked up the phone.

"Roger? Am I disturbing you?"

"You could never disturb me."

"I need to ask you for a favor."

"Go on."

"Do you remember the 100,000 euros I owe my bank?"

"How could I forget? Because of that jerk of a colleague of yours… What's his name?"

"Gianni Pardini."

"That bastard really got you in a mess!"

"Yes, that he did. Now he is in jail. The day before yesterday, for the second time in a month, the bank manager called me, and he wants to see me this week. I sensed from his tone that they want to make me pay all the debt right away. Man, I know you have connections high up in the banking industry. Could you help me find a solution?"

"I'll take care of it, Ben."

"Thanks, man!"

"Don't forget our dinner tomorrow night."

"Thank you for reminding me. Where did you book?"

"The Armani Hotel."

"The Armani? But it's a five-star restaurant!"

"Yes… Of course."

"Roger, you know I can't afford it right now. We can have dinner at my house; my wife—"

"You disappoint me, man; you know that when I invite you, I always pay," he pointed out.

"I know. But my plans don't give me room to spend that much, and I don't feel like going with you all the time when I can't pay for it. This time, man, I can't. Come to my house instead."

"It's my birthday in a week, you know. I was assigned a mission just yesterday and in five days I have to go to Nigeria. I'll be back next month. You are my best friend, and—"

"No. I'll buy you your birthday dinner at my house! Either come or we'll celebrate it when you come back."

"Please!"

"No. No. I'm not coming to the Armani Hotel! I'll see you when you come back."

After this phone call, I felt sad. Roger had just agreed to find a solution to my debt problem, and my friendship with him did not entitle me to treat him like that, especially since he had invited me to that dinner in order to celebrate his birthday with me, his best friend. I immediately called him back to apologize.

"I've changed my mind... Okay, I'll see you tomorrow at the Armani Hotel."

"Great! I'll pick you up at your house!"

The restaurant staff greeted us with reverence, as princes of some oil monarchy. The cashier, the waiters, the dining room manager, all seemed to have known Roger for a long time. I was amazed at how much power money can give. My very dear friend always dined at expensive restaurants. Money had changed him, and I was very sorry about that. "When you have lived in poverty for so long, you choose to fight for the thing from which you can get wealth," he always said. Therefore, his ambition demanded struggle, suffering and toil in order to earn more and more money. Yet even though he loved the good life, he never forgot his friends. His real problem was the way he spent his hard-earned money. With a six-figure annual net income, he thought he could afford everything. He only wore designer clothing – Armani, Gucci, Dolce & Gabbana, Versace. He had taken out a 30-year mortgage to buy a stunning, four-bedroom villa with a swimming pool in Milan. He changed luxury cars at will, leasing BMWs, Audis, and Lexuses, all full option.

The table set for us was decorated with lots of red ribbons scattered here and there with calculated randomness, and a candle diffused a warm light. Soon, the first course arrived: spaghetti and clams, delicious, washed down with an excellent red wine that the solicitous waitress who had been assigned to our table poured into crystal glasses. I took a healthy sip as Roger downed his glass in one drink. Then here was the second course: mixed grilled meat with a salad and chicken rolls with buttered carrots. My friend also virtually devoured the cheeseboard.

As a doctor, I never tired of telling him that his diet was unhealthy and detrimental to his arteries. I repeatedly advised him to eat vegetables, protein, whole grains and unsweetened citrus juices, but he never listened. He did not want to make any effort to return to an acceptable weight. No basketball game with me as in the old days. No gym. No jogging. At this rate, his life was not as enviable as it might have appeared; a heart attack was only a matter of time.

Finally, the birthday cake was served, with two candles in the shape of a 4 and a 5. The waitress and I sang *Happy Birthday* to him, and Roger blew them out while we applauded. Throughout the dinner, we reminisced about our past as students and the changes in our lives since we had started working and earning money, but we also touched on the subject of the future.

20

When we were in college some years ago, after my afternoon classes, I used to stay in the classroom until late to study some more. And so, when I got back to my room, I would almost always find Roger snoring like a trombone. In bed, caught up in my thoughts, I would struggle to fall asleep because I would think about my family, so far away. I had left my father, my mother, my brothers, my sisters, and the rich businessman who had become my 'rich father' and financed my trip. His goodness reassured me, instilled confidence in the future, and I was overjoyed to have met him. This man was younger than my biological father (born poor), but much wiser than he. My father believed that poverty was the supreme virtue, while the businessman, a week before my departure, had hosted me in his mansion for three nights, during which he instructed me on the prosperity that wealth provides, assuring me that if I continued to work steadily on my positive character, the right opportunity would come my way.

"You must persevere, maintain optimism. You must get it into your head that in the face of difficulties and defeats you must not be frightened or stop... ever!"

I had not been frightened even when I was standing in line at the central police headquarters in Via Montebello in Milan to get a residence permit. I had to wait in line at least three hours, amid pushing and insults, among other immigrants. I felt the urge to leave, but I resisted because I needed my residence permit to renew my university registration. When my turn came, a policewoman at the entrance of the building asked me if I had an appointment. I had, and the officer let me through.

There was not a single seat in the large lobby; all the seats were occupied by others like me. An officer handed me a number, and I stood waiting beside the vending machines. I would have made the most of my time there to study human anatomy, but the chatter of workers, street vendors and a few students distracted me.

Every year I would arrive here with my backpack full of college texts, but I couldn't open one to study. Every now and then someone would greet me and then ask me for some advice, a favor, help in getting papers in order, full of ambition and confidence. Then, when the megaphone announced their turn, they would happily go to the counter. There were five officers there taking applications.

A South American woman who was a maid had left angrily because, for the umpteenth time, despite submitting the required documentation, her application had been rejected.

I had to wait my turn, standing, for hours.

I had gone through the same process of renewing my residence permit for three years. Coming to Police Headquarters was an opportunity for me to meet people to whom the West, through the mass media, had conveyed an image of prosperity and happiness. The immigrants were divided into groups: the blacks; the *vu cumprà*, peddlers who sold counterfeit goods of all kinds; the Arabs; the Pakistanis; the South Americans; the Albanians, who were all considered criminals; the Chinese, who opened cafés, restaurants, stores and hair salons everywhere and enslaved their own countrymen. And then the Filipinos, the Indians and the Sinhalese, who assisted the elderly, acted as domestic helpers and dishwashers… And then again, finally, there were trans people and prostitutes of different ethnicities.

A Senegalese man in his 60s approached me. "How are you, brother?" he asked.

"Good. How about you?"

"Very good. How's business?"

"I study at the university. I don't have a business."

"Ah! I am a street vendor and I am fed up with people asking me where I am from and if I am comfortable in Italy. If you answer that you don't fit in, they tell you outright to go back to your country. I like the cuisine, the culture, the people, the lifestyle of this great country, but I don't like—"

"Number 159," announced the megaphone.

I sighed. It was my turn. I introduced myself at counter number five.

"It's too early for your new residence permit."

"Why? I need it for college and—"

"I'm sorry. You have to come back next month."

"It's important for university—"

"I'm sorry; you'll have to come back another time."

"I can't—"

"I'm sorry. I can't do anything about it!"

"But I must have my residence permit. Your boss can—"

"Let me work!"

"Holy crap! I'm a student, not an illegal immigrant! I would like to—"

"Move now! Make way for the next one."

"This is unbelievable! I've been asking for a renewal of my permit for six months! Should I kneel down for—"

"Boy! Goodbye!"

"I can't—"

"So, are you leaving or not?" the policeman shouted. In his view, there was nothing he could do. My fate did not interest him any more than that of others. In addition, the government had recently passed a law allowing illegal immigrants who had been in Italy for more than five years continuously to have a residence permit. I left the counter, and a feeling of humiliation and bewilderment came over me. I went home confused.

21

All afternoon I had been intensely busy in my doctor's office in the hospital. It was a small, neat room. On the wall behind my desk was a poster with a picture of a doctor smiling, arms folded. 'You are in good hands' read the slogan written at the bottom, intended to instill confidence in patients. Volumes on gynecology and obstetrics were placed on various glass shelves. I was talking to a patient – the fifth one that day – who was going to undergo surgery the following day.

"I'm scared, Doctor," the woman said.

"Mrs. Rossi, in almost everything we do, there is risk. Even when we walk down the street, we can get hurt. Living is risky in itself."

"Doctor, are you telling me that there is no such thing as zero risk?"

I had made the decision to always ask the patient whether she felt more comfortable if I called her by her first name or her family name, and from our first meeting this lady told me I could call her by her first name, and I told her she could do the same, if she preferred.

"Yes, Angela, in our clinical practice there is no such thing as zero risk."

"What is the chance of needing a blood transfusion?"

"Two in a hundred women need it after a laparohysterectomy, an abdominal uterine removal, the surgery you're having tomorrow. But that does not mean you'll be one of those women."

"Yes, I understand. When you were handing me the lab test results, you specified that I am a 'high-risk' cervical cancer patient. What does that mean?"

"The liquid-based Pap test with HPV (human papillomavirus) reflex has shown that you are infected with HPV type 18, which we find in 70 percent of cancers of that nature. The high risk indicated by the test does not mean you are definitely going to have cancer. It means that the risk of cancer is greater than 1 in 250 – that is, out of 250 women who test positive for type 18 HPV, more than one develops this tumor. In this situation, after confirmation through colposcopy, I had to propose a hysterectomy, since you are already in menopause."

I had already explained to Angela the status of her illness. A 50-year-old, highly committed and successful lawyer, she had neglected to be screened for cervical cancer for years. The biopsy taken at colposcopy had revealed a grade 1 lesion with a diameter of 2.5 mm and a depth of 6 mm.

Having weighed the different options, the patient had opted for radical treatment, that is, removal of the uterus. Fortunately, the lesion was not more than 3 cm in diameter; otherwise, in addition to the uterus, I would have to remove the ovaries and the lymph nodes and begin radiation therapy. I had arranged for meticulous teamwork. I had informed her as thoroughly as possible about both the tumor and its treatment, and encouraged her to come to me with her husband, who was sitting next to her.

"Do you have any more questions, Angela?"

"No. I am just scared about the surgery tomorrow morning, Doctor."

"I understand, Angela. Don't worry. You are in good hands. Before the surgery I will need you to sign the consent form I gave you last week. It will be a relatively easy surgery. I need you to trust me."

"Yes, I know, Doctor."

"Do you feel ready?"

"I'm ready."

"Good. Then I'll see you tomorrow."

The next day, before taking Mrs. Rossi to the operating room, the anesthesiologist double-checked that everything was in order, and checked the test results and the electrocardiogram on the computer. He made sure the patient had not eaten anything in the past six hours, and examined her mouth to check that there were no removable prostheses that needed to be taken out. While a nurse checked Angela's name band to be sure we were operating on the right patient, I checked with another nurse for any drug allergies, and we confirmed that the procedure listed on the consent form was what we expected. The patient was a Jehovah's Witness and would not accept a blood transfusion, and did not wear contact lenses or jewelry that could pinch a finger or get caught on something. We verified that all the equipment we needed was there. After every detail was checked and double-checked, with the help of my assistants I began the procedure, which lasted about forty-five minutes.

22

I have been in my cell block's gym for half an hour doing weight training. A couple of inmates in gym clothes walk in, greeting me. I return the greeting with a nod; then I see that they start working out using the big pull-up bars, pulling themselves up and down.

More people come in. Three South Americans with tattoos on their faces, including around their eyes, one Italian and two Maghrebi men approach me as I am getting on the treadmill.

A stocky, oval-headed South American with a bad haircut lunges forward and shoves me to the ground.

"Why did you do that?"

"Shut up, you piece of shit!"

"Look," I say, getting to my feet. "I'm not a piece of shit. I demand respect from all of you."

My attackers stare at me; then the Italian, who is taller, with a spiderweb tattoo going up to his neck, picks up a stick and takes a step in my direction.

"I don't understand. Do you, an African, demand respect from me?"

"Yes! Are you the leader?"

He nods at one of his companions, a Moroccan with a crooked nose and pierced right ear, who comes over to me and yells, "You fucking murderer," and gives me a shove. I end up against the treadmill.

"Take it easy. I am not a murderer. I didn't kill anyone!"

"He's lucky, this asshole," says the Moroccan.

"You believe me, then," I blurt out.

"No. For today we won't beat you to death, but you have to give us money!"

The Italian looks at the two men, who for a good minute have stopped training and are watching us. As soon as they meet his eyes, they turn and resume lifting weights. To be honest, the Italian has a terrible look, the kind you don't forget.

He turns his focus back on me and in a challenging manner, with a quietly threatening voice, says, "Come closer, Doctor."

I take a few steps toward him as the four South Americans make room.

"I don't like Africans, but you are not like the others. I believe you when you say you didn't kill that white woman; I believe you, Doctor. I was a worker before I ended up in here, and I worked more than 20 years with Africans. They are quiet people, but inferior to us. Doctor, I am your warranty, your protector."

"My protector?"

"Yes, that's right."

I am trying to figure out something to say to get out of this situation when the Moroccan speaks.

"We all need protection in here."

"What do you mean?" I ask.

"So," the Italian says with a laugh, "I'm your warranty, a big shot, and with me around, no one will bother you."

"A big shot? Like the ones in mafia movies?" I ask in a sardonic tone that annoys him.

"What? Don't test me!" says the Italian.

"Don't insult the boss," barks the Moroccan.

The South American grabs my arm and starts squeezing. It hurts like hell, but I try to remain unfazed.

"Leave him," his boss orders him.

It's like having a limb released from a press. I would like to massage it, but I have to remain still, immovable and impassive.

"Let's talk money," resumes the Moroccan.

"7,000 euros. Doctor, you now owe us 7,000 euros," the boss states.

"For what?"

"For not getting killed in here! And if someone breaks your arm or leg, we'll retaliate."

"No deal."

"7,000 euros is a lot of money. I'll give you time to put it together."

"You are dreaming."

"I'll give you ten days."

"Like I said, no deal."

The boss grins with his back to me.

"Okay, Doctor. I actually don't give a damn whether

you're in or not. You just have to bring me the money. I have some guards working for me and they will get it for me. I want it in ten days. Period. If I don't see it in ten days, I'll cut your dick off and have your wife shot in the head. Or I'll have her raped, and as for you, I'll have you shot in the head."

The threat is quite clear. I take in the threatening glances of those present. The boss pushes me violently and I fall to the ground. He points to the door. The Moroccan opens it, and before escorting the Italian out of the gym, one of the South Americans says, "Don't ever talk to the boss like that again. Because if you do it again, I swear it won't be him who kills you – it will be me, with my own hands!"

23

The last surgery in the operating room ran an hour late. Leaving my office, I hurriedly took the elevator to the parking lot and drove home as fast as I could. The first thing I did when I arrived was hug my wife.

"Sorry I'm late, Hat!"

She kissed me on the lips. She was already ready to go out; we were going to have dinner out. She was wearing an emerald green dress and looked gorgeous. Every time I looked at her I felt a slight jolt, a mixture of love and desire.

"Hurry up, honey."

"What about the children?"

"They're fine in their room. They've already had dinner."

"I'm going to take a shower right now."

After the shower, I put on my suit and tie and went into my children's room. I found them in the bunk bed. While Naturi was lying on the bottom bed, yawning, her brother Kemi was sitting on the top, cross-legged, with a cell phone in his hand. They knew today was a special day for Mom and Dad and that every year we celebrated it by going out to dinner, if my job permitted.

I told them to 'be good' because the person we had called to stay with them until midnight was running slightly late, and I kissed them goodnight. I was about to leave the room when I heard ringing. It was the babysitter.

We got to the restaurant at 9pm on the dot; they set us up at a table by the window, overlooking the Naviglio. The towpath was packed with people walking by. Come to think of it, it was the first time we had dined there.

"I thought I would try a little change. Their specialty is fish. When I called to make a reservation, they told me they have shrimp, and I know you love them!" said Hat.

I reached across the table and gave her a sweet, intense kiss.

"Thank you. You are a wonderful wife."

"Happy anniversary, my wonderful husband."

The dinner was exquisite. We were celebrating our first kiss, which my wife had only granted me when we were about to make love for the first time. Hat always remembered that day because she said it had been wonderful.

"That day I discovered what it is to make love, and it was beautiful just because of you!" she would say. At that time, she was still a virgin.

Half an hour after we arrived at the restaurant, my wife received a message on WhatsApp. It was from Kemi.

"Bye Mom and Dad. Have fun!"

It was followed by the emoji of the smiley face with the little heart-shaped eyes.

"Thank you, little man. Mommy and Daddy love you. You and your sister mean the world to us."

My wife added the big red heart emoji.

During the evening we discussed our future. I told her about my plans, and she sat listening, sipping her red wine and looking into my eyes. I was happy to be there too, listening to her tell me about her satisfactions and more: her life as a woman and as a mother had presented her with some difficulties, yet she talked to me about them with the same air of defiance that had made me fall in love with her so strongly, years before.

24

The morning of my Audi fire, I was forced to take the subway to Loreto to get to the hospital. Because I was not hungry, I had left the house without eating breakfast while Hat and the children were still sleeping. I had 12 appointments at the hospital and was scheduled to visit my first patient at 7.30. I hurried down the stairs; then, still hurrying, I bought and stamped my ticket and, without stopping, took the escalator to the green line train. The doors were closing but I quickly pushed myself into the carriage. I felt sluggish. It had been a while since I had taken public transportation; I was no longer used to it. Even though I was standing, I closed my eyes and let myself be lulled by the buzz of passengers' conversations in different languages.

When I opened them again, I found myself in front of a guy who was looking at me with an expressionless smile. I knew that kind of smile from my time as an immigrant in Italy. We were both standing there. We looked at each other for a moment. Then suddenly, without warning, the guy asked me, "Where are you from?" Oh no! Not that! I wasn't angry. If anything, I was tired. Perhaps any normal person would be tired of hearing the same music for more than 25 years, but the only thing I cared about at that moment was getting to the hospital to take care of my patients. I didn't want to pander to the curiosity of a person I had never met before and who was calling me '*tu*' (an Italian word for 'you' that, used to address an adult stranger, is condescending) with devious arrogance.

"I'm from the Loreto stop," I replied.

"What African country are you from?" he asked, pushing.

"From Mars!" I replied.

Meanwhile, the people around us had grown more interested in our conversation, and the guy realized that I was making fun of him. I was rather annoyed by the brutality of his questions.

"Don't fuck with me! Senegal. You're Senegalese, aren't you?" the guy asked, in an increasingly aggressive tone.

General dismay. There is nothing wrong with wanting to know someone's background. But there are other ways to approach the issue, I think. If you want to get to know a person whose origins interest you, you have to take into account the fact that someone may be rather hesitant to confide in a stranger.

"One could also say I was Chinese!" I replied.

A young South American woman standing not far from me burst out laughing. When the train came to a stop, the would-be Lieutenant Colombo had time to hiss before getting off, "Fucking negro!"

Some people will always remain ignorant, I thought. The carriage filled up and the journey resumed. A girl had gotten on with a newspaper, and I found myself behind her. I lowered my eyes to the page she was reading. An advertisement announced, "Your gifts help us fight poverty..."

Many people do not know that racial capitalism was born at the end of the 17th century with the fusion of the concepts of race and capitalism, which first expressed itself in the African slave trade. Before the discovery of America, and consequently the commodification of the African man, slavery had existed for thousands of years, with Europeans getting their slaves from Slavic and Balkan populations. The theory of the inferiority of the African man descends directly from the doctrine of racial capitalism.

We all see posters with undernourished children photographed in African slums. Very often they are posted at the entrance to a bank, a busy public place, a church; we see them in newspapers or on TV or the internet. They are visions that arouse sadness and compassion. The African child is most often naked, dirty, hungry, ghostly thin. Almost always in the image there appears a European missionary or benefactor with a messiah-like attitude.

It is propaganda.

Most people experience the fight against poverty as if it were a drug, thinking that it is a fatal disease, without ever questioning those who would have us believe that almost all Africans know only hunger and AIDS, that misery is the only reality in a continent full of oil, gold, diamonds and so on.

When I lived in Don Pietro's community, it was clear that my freedom had been expropriated. I felt as if I were in a prison because I could not do anything I liked, and I had to accept abuse just because I was African. I was not the creator and protagonist of my destiny, but rather was in a cage.

The 'fight against poverty' is the best propaganda for racial capitalism. I have always projected in my mind's eye the following images in a flashing, rapid film sequence of 60 seconds, trying not to think in terms of good and evil or right and wrong, but rather considering how familiar these scenes are to us in the reality projected every day in the mass media, and especially on television.

The image of a starving African child with a swollen belly, skeletal body, stands out on the screen while a patronizing voice pleads for money to save him through some Western humanitarian association promoting a 'solidarity' campaign.

The corner of an African village full of shacks surrounded by a desolate landscape.

A starving African man, his dishonored and gaunt body magnified on the screen, while, again, a patronizing voice asks for money to save him through a Western humanitarian association that promotes a so-called 'solidarity' campaign.

On the 8pm news, an African child-soldier holds a machine gun in his hands and rejoices in front of the body of an African man he has so coldly shot down with his firearm.

African presidents and leaders who have successfully studied in Paris, London, New York and Milan, and who always dress in suits and ties, running their countries from luxurious palaces.

Orphanages filled with African children of all ages looking for European families ready to adopt them.

Zoomed-in images of poor teenagers with swollen bellies caused by malnutrition, pregnant teenage girls, 14-year-old boys dressed in ripped jeans that hang below their buttocks.

African successes in the West: Samuel Eto'o, Didier Drogba, Angelique Kidjo, Manu Dibango and other artists and soccer players who all serve as role models and heroes.

Tattooed African rappers who perform shirtless; African women dancers who shake their butts to the rhythm of music; and African comedians who are incredibly funny but who are, however, selected only for their shows that reinforce the stereotype of the lesser African.

Naomi Campbell, seductive at a fashion show in Milan.

Lewis Hamilton winning Formula 1 at Maranello.

Michael Jordan flying through the air to make a basket.

Yvonne Chaka Chaka singing about love.

Workers wearing tattered clothes, working hard, stressed and underpaid but smiling as they stand on a coffee plantation, with the words 'We are defenders of the land of Africa' on the screen.

Blank faces of neglected and abandoned elderly

people, of emaciated adults and obese or malnourished children in the land of plenty, Africa, all sick due to diets that are poor or composed of junk food, from diabetes, heart disease, AIDS and other diseases that could be prevented but have long been ignored in Africa.

An urban school similar to a run-down factory with armed guards.

A teacher in an overcrowded classroom who attempts to instruct the children without books or the necessary means to take notes.

A photo gallery: Thurgood Marshall, Martin Luther King Jr. and other Black History Month politicians and dignitaries in America.

The reel ends with 'We are the change we seek'. Dominating the screen is a glorious photo of Barack Obama with first lady Michelle at his side. Fading black-and-white images with the voice of the 44th president of the world's most powerful nation repeating the now-familiar phrase: "It is our time!"

After viewing my film, I snap back to reality, but not before the memory of the night before my departure from Laa'Si' comes back to me.

*

Early in the morning, those who had attended my farewell party greeted me, telling me that the greatest virtue is generosity: one must give without expecting anything in return.

I made my way back at a good pace, stopping only at

noon to eat, sitting under a tree, pausing for only half an hour, eating, with enjoyment, half the abundant supply of food the women had placed in my bag.

Continuing on, I walked for hours and was passing through a vineyard when dusk began to fall; so, coming to an open, secluded cottage, I stopped. Inside was equipment for harvesting coffee, nothing else. There was no one there. I thought it was a suitable place to spend the night and decided to collect some wood in the vicinity. In my pocket I still had plenty of matches, which on the way to Laa'Si' had enabled me to light a fire in the cave, and soon I was lighting a hearty fire here as well; it produced cheerful crackles and gave off light and warmth.

I yawned and lay down beside the fire. I remained awake for a long time pondering this question: why do the countries of the world have different capacities for economic development? In my opinion, for several reasons, mainly including the systems of government, the laws that regulate the economy, and the incentives that motivate individuals. Inclusive economic institutions are those that encourage wealth by giving individuals, supported by the state, the power to choose. By contrast, in my home community, economic institutions are prone to be used by certain social groups to appropriate the income and wealth produced by others, creating mass poverty. Thomas Edison, Bill Gates, Larry Page, Jeff Bezos and hundreds of rich people exist because Western society recognizes their freedom to express their talents by creating the conditions for them to materialize. There are not many Bill Gateses and Albert Einsteins in Sub-

Saharan Africa because, just as happened with slavery, colonization and neocolonialism, African heads of state also subjugate and impoverish their people. On this God-blessed continent, many families do not have the financial means to send their children to school, and in any case, the quality of education leaves something to be desired; teachers often do not feel like working and do not show up to class, or books go missing.

The fire was down to its last glow when I finally managed to drift off to sleep. I awoke at dawn, and the small bonfire was now only cold, gray ash. I left the cottage and resumed my trek toward Bayangam.

25

"Who?"

"Bacol. He is Albanian."

We are in our cell. Mattia is lying on his back on the bed, his head resting on the pillow. Earlier I told him about my encounter at the gym with the Italian and his gang of foreigners. He knows they gave me ten days to come up with 7,000 euros.

"Are you sure he's the right person?"

"Very sure. In here, when Bacol is with you, everyone leaves you alone. He doesn't take care only of his community. If he makes a commitment, he gets good results. Let me talk to him, and you'll see that things will work out."

"Where will we meet him to talk?"

"Occasionally Bacol goes out into the courtyard to get some air. When we see each other, we usually don't say anything; we just exchange a nod. Very rarely he greets me and asks how I am."

I have confidence in Mattia. I have shared with him all the information I got from Andrea.

"Barbara was killed. No, it's not a bad dream. It really happened, and I was there. They say I am the murderer as she was my lover. How can I prove my innocence and find the real killer if I'm locked up in here?" I ask him, at my wits' end.

I don't know what to do. I can't get Barbara's bloody face out of my head, her blood running through my fingers and my hands, unable to stop it.

"Let's use our imaginations, try to think of some scenarios. First scenario: someone gives the order to eliminate you. Where do you imagine the meeting between Suardi and Monti took place?"

"What do you think?"

"In a parking lot. I see Monti driving his car. He stops and turns off the engine. It is eleven o'clock. After he sits there in the dark for ten minutes, listening to music, Suardi approaches, ducking down to check who is in the car as Monti opens the door. Suardi gets in and Monti turns off the music. 'Well?' says Monti. 'Let's proceed.'

"'I'm ready,' replies Suardi. Monti reaches behind him, takes an envelope from the back seat and hands it to Suardi.

"'There's what we agreed on,' he says, 'and I explained to you yesterday what you have to do. Don't make a mistake.'

"'I never make mistakes,' Suardi replies.

"'You must kill him without mercy.'"

"I don't think that's what happened at all. I am still alive, and Barbara was killed!"

"Second hypothesis: Mr. Monti is acting alone. I see—"

"Let me stop you right there, my friend. That theory doesn't hold up. He can't be the killer. The man who attacked me was strong, tall and muscular."

"Third scenario: it was a crime of passion. The victim was dating a man who found out she didn't love him and wanted to leave him for you. That is enough for a fool in love to kill the woman he loves."

"All right. What else do we need to know?"

"The murder was premeditated. He often came to Barbara's house, had the keys, entered the house at that time and found her sleeping…"

"No, Barbara was not in her pajamas; she was wearing a yellow cardigan."

"Ah! Let's say they had dinner together in the house, then Barbara told him she loved someone else. He insisted on knowing who it was, and Barbara, forced, confessed to him that it was you."

"That makes sense, except I never dated that woman!"

"It doesn't matter whether you dated her. The truth is, she was crazy about you, and that's all that matters. The killer told her to call you."

"Which she did."

"You ran straight to her, didn't you?"

"True."

"Why?"

"I don't know."

"Okay. Don't you find it strange that he didn't kill you too?"

"Very strange. I don't understand why."

"Do you think it was luck?"

"Eww…"

"What? Not luck?"

"No, luck is needed in life. Suck is all I got. They locked me up even though I didn't have a motive for killing her…"

"I'm sorry, man. We've only known each other a short time, but I know you're innocent. As I understand it, you never dated Barbara."

"That's right."

"There's also another possibility: that Barbara owed money to drug dealers with whom she did business."

"I'm a little confused by all these scenarios. I need to talk to my lawyer to find out what he is doing."

26

I am talking to Andrea from the prison payphone. I imagine him sitting behind his desk in his office.

"No. The police investigation ruled that out: Barbara did not do drugs. She did not deal. She did not belong to the world of drug trafficking."

"I see. What leads are you following now?"

"Cameras. We are checking the cameras in the vicinity of the crime scene for images of the killer or the black Ford Fiesta."

"Do you think the murderer left any traces?"

"You never know. One thing is certain: Suardi's Ford was parked in front of the café-restaurant where Barbara worked for five nights before the day of the murder."

"He knew where she worked?" I ask.

"Exactly, Ben, which means that in all probability Barbara knew her killer. That said, there is something that escapes me…"

"What?"

"If I knew, I wouldn't say it escapes me. Something in the camera frames – I can't make out the person getting out of the Ford. But one thing is certain…"

"What, Andrea?"

"He's hiding something, and I want to find out what before I take this evidence to the police."

"You do this a lot, don't you?"

"Do what?"

"Act prudently – find the culprit and then go to the police, and also to the press."

"Then you know how I work!"

"I know you are very good at what you do."

"Thank you, friend; your trust gives me the determination to catch this killer. I'll see you tomorrow at ten o'clock. We will talk, among other things, about your car being set on fire."

"Why? I guess you found out who the arsonist is," I say, but my lawyer has already put down the phone.

I stand there for a few moments, staring at the receiver I am clutching, as the memory of the fire comes back to me.

On that day, shortly after 6pm, after circling around for 15 minutes, I was lucky enough to be able to park on a narrow, deserted street. I noticed that there were no security cameras or blue lines. I wandered around for an hour or so and went in several stores to take a look. I was in a bookstore in Corso Buenos Aires when my cellphone rang. It was a *carabiniere*.

"Are you Dr. Ben Kom?" he asked.

"Yes, I am."

"Do you know where your car is?"

"I parked it just now, nearby."

"It has been set on fire, Doctor."

"What?"

"Your car was set on fire!"

"My car?"

"Yes, Doctor, your car. Come right away. The fire department is on the job."

When I arrived at the scene, I found that my Audi had been badly damaged by the fire that the firefighters had now extinguished. I introduced myself and showed my ID to the *carabinieri*.

"Doctor, we are initiating investigations into the cause of the fire that developed in the engine compartment. We need to know whether it was an accident or arson. The damage is to be quantified."

It was immediately clear to me that it was arson. I wondered if Monti, Mrs. Rivera's husband, was the arsonist. I have never forgotten his words: "I swear I will make you pay for this… you bastard!"

The next day, I woke up at dawn. It was bitterly cold outside; the windowpanes were white with frost. It was the first time I had forgotten to lower the shutter even though, before she fell asleep, Hat had reminded me to close it.

I slept badly. I wondered angrily who could have set my car on fire. Was Mr. Monti punishing me for saving his wife's life and failing to prevent her from becoming infertile? But after all, they already had a child!

So many times I had wondered how this guy would get revenge. Ever since the racist threat was written on my apartment building, I had been asking myself a thousand questions. Was it the work of one or more racists? Would they perhaps hurt me and my loved ones? The police had not found the culprit or culprits. This worried me. And when I am worried, I feel strange: I fight to push fear away, to win my freedom, absolutely rejecting defeat. I fight and fight and fight with all my spiritual energy; but sometimes I am tired, even of that.

27

Four hundred men live in this prison, and almost half will have to spend the rest of their lives here. Bacol is one of those who have no doubt that they will end up in Hell when they die.

The 60-year-old Albanian summoned me to the prison laundry room, where he has been working for a decade. Before this, he carried groceries and packages from one part of San Vittore to another. Besides officially sorting the inmates' uniforms, he deals with human desperation by controlling the drug business. His rules are quite simple. Never buy from anyone other than one of his dealers. Don't do or say anything that he might consider a betrayal. Do not be a mole or rat out another inmate for any reason in the world. And, above all, his rule number one, which must never, ever be broken: don't do anything wrong when you are under his protection. Already being naturally violent, he becomes especially so as a godfather.

"From now on I am your protector. Do you know what that means?"

"Yes. I know your rules, Bacol."

"Boss. You call me Boss! I'll forgive you this time."

Anyone who requests his protection must call him 'Boss', my cellmate told me, otherwise the Albanian will get angry and become violent.

Like me, he wears a prison uniform. He fixes his gaze on me. I try to radiate calmness, hoping to instill it in him.

"What the hell are you staring at me for, Doctor? Why aren't you afraid of me?"

"I respect you, but I'm not afraid of you!" I reply.

"You should be!" says Bacol, known as Rambo – not only because he has a machine gun and the word 'BOSS' tattooed on his forearm, but also because he is about six feet tall, with a shaved head and a bodybuilder's physique. He has been a mercenary and arms dealer for African countries at war. He proudly tells me about his adventures in the African jungles. He lets me know that he was involved in a confrontation several times, and he killed several Africans with his machine gun. He still cannot understand why the weapons-of-war lobby abandoned him soon after the conflict in Angola ended. He was arrested in Africa and deported to Albania, where he was sentenced to 15 years in prison, but after six months he escaped. With accomplices, he managed to get to Italy, where he raped and killed five women in three different regions just because those poor women had the misfortune of crossing his path.

The Milan courts sentenced him to life in prison.

"You should fear me, Doctor! Let's make a deal: you pay nothing for the protection I offer, and in return you become my personal doctor! You know, Doctor, I've been hypertensive for five years, and I've been told I also have diabetes. Do you agree?"

"Agreed." I cannot do otherwise. Better than finding myself paying money or risking my life in prison.

"Is there an update from the police on your case?"

Bacol seemed to know as much as Mattia.

"Apparently Barbara and that other guy, Monti, knew each other. According to my lawyer they were dating. Maybe Barbara was doing it a little bit for money, prostituting herself. Or maybe they loved each other…"

"Your cellmate told me your story, and my opinion is that a woman who loves you so much does not sell herself to another man."

"I'm just repeating what my lawyer said," I explain. "That's all."

"You don't… You never really… I mean…"

"No. I have never made love to her."

"I believe you… In the past I have had ties to neo-Nazi or extremist groups. I know people who know people. I became a good guy. Of course, I had my troubles with them…"

"Did you hate Africans?"

Bacol nods. "Yes, but we are talking about the distant past."

"What changed your mind?"

"My wife. She was African, from Mozambique. I met her more than 20 years ago, during the war, and we fell in love. I lost her and our son."

"Ah, I'm sorry – how did that happen?"

Bacol's hand closes into a fist, squeezing the fabric of the uniform above the laundry table between his fingers.

"Racists from my country took her away from me. Princess was her name. We got married six months after my first mercenary contract in Mozambique. We got married in Tirana, my hometown in Albania. Then I went back to the war, leaving my wife with my family. She was three months pregnant when three white neo-Nazis killed her with six gunshots to the chest as she was coming out of a supermarket with my sister. She died instantly, with my child in her womb. We were very close…"

"I see."

"Enough about me… The cops claim it was you who slit the woman's throat. No one has been able to say exactly who phoned the police. Did you buy the cell phone the call came from?"

"No."

"So, someone who knows you well and wants to ruin you must have done it! A friend?"

"A friend? Apart from my lawyer, I have only one friend. Roger."

"Is he capable of…"

"No. He could never, ever hurt anyone."

"Not even out of jealousy?"

"He didn't do it. I know that. Besides, why would he be jealous of me?"

"I don't know."

"You're just mistaken. Roger is more than a friend; he is a brother to me."

28

At midnight, Roger parked his BMW near the run-down residential buildings with their crumbling facades, leaving the engine running. We were on Via Padova; I was sitting in the front passenger seat. From a first-floor balcony we could hear laughter, and we could also hear people speaking Spanish – a group of South American boys and girls – and salsa and merengue music blaring.

While much of Milan slept deeply, the street in the Nolo district vibrated with life.

On the street, a very comely young woman was talking to a man. She had a beautiful cheerful face, black hair that ran down the length of her back, and red lips.

In front of an Egyptian kebab shop, a dozen people were sitting at outdoor tables smoking hookahs, chatting in Arabic and Italian. A dog lying under one of the tables in a café slept blissfully.

In the Cuzco brewery, customers were speaking

Spanish, bottles in hand.

Customers of all nationalities were coming out of the Chinese restaurant that offered all-you-can-eat.

As I turned my head toward Roger to thank him for a wonderful evening, I was taken aback by the fact that, at 45, my friend looked 60. He had a face full of wrinkles, evidence of a reckless and excess-laden life. He had lost the sense of humor he had in college, seemed to have become incapable of laughing, and his eyes were full of sadness.

"How are you always able to stay so slim and handsome? I could never do it…"

"Wanting is power, man," I interrupt him. "You spend your time complaining about your appearance, claiming that you can't change it. Professionally, you have reached the highest levels. Why don't you strive to do the same with your health?"

"No, I know; I'll try…"

"All right, man. Tomorrow, unfortunately I can't accompany you to the airport, but when you get back I'll be there to pick you up. Again, thanks for dinner and for driving me home," I concluded.

Just what I had always feared happened on his return from Nigeria. Roger was having a heart attack, lying on the ground, his overweight body wrapped in an Armani suit. I asked a woman who was nearby to call 118, then noticed that he was not breathing and his heart was no longer beating, so I immediately started CPR. One, two, three, four, five… I was so engrossed in the maneuver that I did not hear the EMTs arriving. They quickly got to work on him while a nurse whispered words of comfort, although I doubt he could hear them.

The worst was over. Death had been defeated, and almost two weeks later, after surgery, Roger was in a single room in the ICU of the cardiology operating unit.

My colleagues in cardiology had informed me that the patient was clinically stable. He was regaining his health. He had not needed infusions for a few days. A nurse measured his temperature and blood pressure four times a day.

Sitting on the small chair next to the bed, I could see her handling the instruments swiftly and confidently, and gently fastening the band around his arm. Then I heard the puff of air from the rubber pump, and shortly thereafter the hiss of air escaping.

"Parameters are within normal range," the nurse informed me. I merely thanked her with a nod of my head.

I visited Roger every day. Not always at the same time, but whenever I finished work and had some time, I would go to see him. It had been more than two months since he had recovered. I missed him; I missed his almost daily short phone calls, always at the least opportune times, to make small talk of no importance – at least for me, who was always busy with work.

"Man, it's a shitty day."

"Roger, I'm with a patient. I can't talk right now."

"I just wanted to tell you that I'm having a difficult day at work."

Roger had a very good wife, Susan, whom I always found beside him when I visited. Sometimes she would also bring their two children. When I arrived, I would tell her to go home, especially when I noticed that she had spent the night in the hospital and I would find her curled up on the little chair beside the bed.

"I can tell you are very tired; go home and rest! The children need you."

Once she was gone, I was left alone in the room with my friend.

"Roger... Can you hear me?" I whispered in his ear.

He pulled his arm out from under the covers to give me an awkward, affectionate hug.

"Thank you!" he said.

'Thank you' is not a phrase that should be uttered to only a select few. I say it every day, every time I wake up, before I get out of bed. Then immediately afterwards I allow my mind to be invaded by the beauty of the things I wish to have and accomplish. When I focus on the present moment, I am happy. My thoughts are transformed, taking shape in four dimensions.

"Visualizing an event before it happens is possible for those who can access this dimension," my rich father had taught me. "Everything we project in that world will happen in this world, which is three-dimensional."

"How is that possible?" I asked him. My rich father gave a slight smile. I knew well that it was not out of amusement, but out of his certainty that every man has within himself the potential to create his own future.

"The key thing to consider is that our future is flexible. It depends more on how we think and our habits than on our actions. We are the idea we have of ourselves. All changes take place in the thoughts we think. Our imagination, when controlled – that is, governed by desire – merges with the past and future into one present. Thus, the spiritual man knows how to make material in the physical world what is immaterial in thought."

"Wonderful!" I replied. In time, I really came to understand what he meant, and it became a habit for me to say every morning, "Thank you! I am so happy and grateful because I am in perfect health. I have love for myself, for my family, and for the people I meet. Thank you for the money that I am earning that allows me to live in this beautiful house and not lack anything."

As I say these words I begin to smile, feeling joy at the idea of the simple things that happen to me during the day. I certainly do not have doubts. Being happy is the choice I make every morning, which is why after the initial "Thank you!" I continue my thoughts with the word 'happy'. My cheeks always light up with sincere enthusiasm, and I know that I am about to achieve many positive goals. Instead of being too busy doing, focusing on the difficulties I encounter, I rejoice in my strength and ability to add value to the lives of others, and I am grateful. I do not think about what I lack but try to focus on what I have achieved by my actions and will. In doing so, what I desire becomes living matter, something concrete that evolves and offers feedback for my happiness. Thinking intensely about something only attracts positive events that in turn make it happen. It is a universal law!

There are circumstances that require us to reflect on our lives and how to improve them. Illness is one of them.

"If he really loved himself, he would no longer neglect his health as he has so far," Susan told me as she clasped the hands of her five- and seven-year-old children.

They had just gotten off the elevator in the hospital's main lobby when we met. We stopped to talk for a few minutes.

"Pull yourself together," I said, hugging her tightly. Susan nodded skeptically: she doubted that her husband would willingly give up unhealthy habits, but she would push him towards a healthy and better future.

Susan is of Nigerian descent and a devout Christian, a very determined woman who has always taken her children to church on Sunday. The children attend catechism in the parish and are present at all social activities. Despite her extravagant life, she has always taken good care of her husband by not keeping alcoholic beverages in the house or feeding him overly fatty and salty dishes. However, she was never able to convince him to devote time to meditation and prayer.

I wondered if Roger was going to understand that he had to hold on tightly to his wonderful wife. I kissed the children on the forehead.

"I'm going up to see him," I said as we parted.

I took the elevator to the second floor, the location of the Cardiac Rehabilitation Operating Unit, to which Roger had been transferred a week before. His new room was halfway down the hall. It was the third time in a week that I had gone in there. The window curtains were open. Roger was sitting up in bed. The television was tuned to a non-stop news channel, but the volume was too low to hear reporters' commentaries on the tug-of-war between

North Korea and the U.S. over nuclear weapons. The sick man put down the crossword puzzle that he had been filling in with a pencil in order to receive the two kisses that I was about to give him on the cheeks. I noticed a penknife, an eraser and a rosary resting on a Bible next to a nearly full glass of water. Susan had made it clear to Roger that God felt it was too soon for him to leave, and that their marriage did not deserve to end this way. This time, Roger seemed to understand.

"I can see that you are experiencing the presence of the Divine Essence in you!" I said, before settling down in the chair by the bed.

"I have seen death up close, man. I say 'thank you' to the creator of all things, who evidently loves me," he admitted.

"Now you have to simplify your life, and together we have to find some answers. Everything happens for a reason. What is the purpose of this? What lesson does it hold? What is the real meaning of our lives?"

"How is work going?" he asked, changing the subject.

"Great, Roger."

He and I talked about everything; there were no secrets between us.

"It is so important for you, for me, for your African brothers, that you become a chief physician!"

"Thank you. In fact, I will become one; I am preparing for the competition, and I will win it."

"Yes, you will win it!"

Everything was clear in my mind. Every time I closed my eyes, I saw myself as chief physician at the hospital.

29

I feel as if the walls of the visiting room are crushing me. In my head I am a free man, but in reality my lawyer is informing me that the case has suffered a setback: his requests to have the forensic report have been denied by the police. Italy does not have the death penalty, but for such a vicious murder, there is no judge that would sentence me to less than 15 years in prison. I now see that my career is over and the hell of solitary confinement in prison, probably for life, is looming before me as in a movie where I am the protagonist. It is hard to think of happiness, of gratitude, under such dramatic conditions.

"I still haven't been able to understand why the victim's neighbor is accusing you of being the murderer. My staff and I are following leads, and there are people involved."

"Andrea, I don't know what new evidence Barbara's neighbor has provided to the police, but it's definitely bullshit. The person who murdered that woman is free; everything else is rubbish."

Andrea does not reply but seems surprised by my aggressive tone. I reiterate forcefully, "And you need to get me out of here!"

"Ben," Andrea says, trying to calm me down, "my team is on the job for you and we will find the culprit. You can trust Sarah!"

My lawyer's optimism is like a breath of fresh air for me. He talks about the physical evidence, indicating that some of it actually exonerates me. My incarceration is nothing more than an abuse of power. He is basically telling me that the police, especially Chief Inspector Trebano, are refusing to cooperate with the defense and are intentionally withholding evidence.

"What exactly are we talking about?" I ask.

"DNA," Andrea replies. "A few days ago I insisted that a new inspection be made at the crime scene, and in the closet we found the clothing and personal effects of a man. The chief inspector collected them following procedure and handed them over to the forensic police, who put them through the serology protocol."

"You're telling me that…"

"Hair has been found; the DNA does not match Barbara's."

"And whom does it belong to?"

"I don't know. The police wouldn't tell me, and I still haven't been able to get the full forensic report. Apparently they want to exhibit it only during the trial, if of course the judge requests it."

"It could be Suardi's DNA, right?"

"No," Andrea replied. "Suardi has never been in that apartment and never met Barbara."

"How—?"

"He has an alibi: at the time of the murder, he was in Caserta. He got back to Milan the next day."

"Do you really believe that?"

"We have made all the possible checks, which indicate that Barbara and Suardi did not know each other and had never communicated."

"What about his black Ford Fiesta parked in front of the place where Barbara worked?"

"We're not sure if he was behind the wheel. However, we'll know soon enough."

"For me, it's Monti who somehow engineered the whole thing. I'm sure of that."

"Ben... you know we've thought about it; we've looked at several hypotheses, but we can't prove it."

"Who else could have killed that poor woman?"

"We don't know for sure yet. Look at this video."

At a nod of consent from the prison officer, the lawyer takes out his cell phone and shows me a clip.

"This is the Bunga Club," he says. "Barbara used to go there a lot."

This is a very famous and coveted nightclub in the center of Milan. It is located inside a deconsecrated church. Security protocols include video surveillance at the entrance, with footage recorded and stored in a special room. And that footage has been downloaded onto Andrea's phone.

"This is not the first time the Bunga Club has cooperated with me. When Sarah found out that the victim went there every week, I asked to see the footage prior to the murder," Andrea explains.

Three bouncers can be seen, two black and one white, stepping aside to let Barbara leave first. She is wearing a fashionable red dress and high heels; behind her is a tall, handsome man with a hint of a beard, fine features, and dark hair parted on the side. He is wearing a smart gray suit. Just outside the disco they kiss passionately, looking so in love that they can't keep their hands off each other, his fingers sliding between her thighs.

"Jesus Christ! Who is that man?" I ask.

"We don't know yet."

"Does it belong to him?" I ask.

"What?" retorts Andrea.

"The DNA."

"We don't know!"

"From the footage, it's easy to guess."

"We are waiting to get hold of the forensic report."

"All right. Now what happens?"

"This is a new lead we are investigating. We need to find the man in the film. We know he lives in Milan. I have to tell you something else, Ben."

"I'm listening."

"We are in contact with the store that sold the phone from which the killer called the police."

"Wonderful."

"My staff and I are talking to people who will help us."

"Thank you, Andrea. If you weren't here to defend me..."

I do not get to finish the sentence when Andrea looks into my eyes, suddenly pale, frightened. He has something to tell me that deep down I already know.

"Ten days," he says.

"What does that mean?"

"The hearing is in ten days. That's how much time I have left to find the real culprit."

"Andrea, I trust you! I know you will solve this case."

"I will, because, besides knowing that you are innocent, I believe in justice. 'Better a hundred guilty men go free than one innocent man rots in jail' is my motto."

30

I had told myself a story about the freedom I would find in Italy. I dreamed of the lavish lifestyle I had seen on television and the freedom of a democratic society. My thoughts were focused on fighting all forms of servility; with pride and boldness, I wanted to assert my right to an independent and opulent existence.

But the kind of life that Don Pietro had in store for me, that he had built for 'his Africans', as he called us, had me going through days filled with unhappiness. I had instinctively trusted that priest, a bit like the way one trusts a martial arts master. He fitted me into a pre-established regimen of daily tasks and duties in which the only thing that mattered was the community. The community and that was it.

In both developed and developing countries, people who do not suffer injustice very often say that a poor person can only be saved by humanitarian aid. According to them, generosity to the poor is a mission, a human experience of faith and love.

"The poor must let us help them, accept our goodness and give thanks," I have read many times between the lines in newspapers. However, I have never found the truth written anywhere, which is that only trade between countries promotes development, overcomes poverty and brings justice to the world.

I would like to tell all the dear Don Pietros something they may not have imagined: Africa is not poor by choice. Someone, some self-centered system, has exercised its power over a vast continent based on a supposed superiority. We are told that destiny wanted African man to be born destitute because he does not have the means to lead an easy existence; we are told that cockroaches, rats and mosquitoes invade the African ecosystem. We are children of illiterate peasants; we are descendants of irresponsible fathers; we are beings who never became part of the History of Mankind and who do not matter. We are seen and labeled only in this way, as if we were objects.

If someone were to ask me to tell them who I really am, then I might start from World War II, when my father, at only seventeen years of age, was picked up by the French, along with thousands of other Africans, and sent to Normandy to fight the Germans. Africans at that time were part of Human History because they were useful in defeating Hitler. They fought, with many dying, and triumphed over the Nazis. But after the Allied victory, Dad and all the other Africans were sent home like parcels, without a thank you or financial reward. An injustice he never complained about.

I have always been convinced, however, that I was

not born to work for others, neither in a servile and mechanical way nor in any other way! I like freedom, and above all I want to have the ability to say no when I see fit.

Always saying yes and smiling even when they offend you with racist epithets, even when they exploit you, is a dangerous first step toward servitude and creates an inferiority complex that becomes impossible to get rid of. Don Pietro's supposed altruism made me feel uncomfortable, and prevented me from living on an equal footing with others by instilling a tendency to devalue myself.

"I am taking care of your education, so you must do as I say!" said Don Pietro, blackmailing me with his Christian charity.

Because at one point I realized that putting my head in the sand would only make my situation worse, I began to display a certain bravado.

The serenity I sought I found only in Franca's company. In church and in the cafeteria, she wanted me to sit by her side. When she met me in the morning, she would greet me with a good morning kiss on the lips, as if blowing a word of love. When I kissed her on the cheeks, her mouth sought mine more than once, making my heart beat faster. I would fall asleep dreaming of her smile and her curves highlighted by her light clothes. I desperately craved that woman, who, I now realize, was trying to seduce me. When I saw her I felt intense desire, but I restrained myself because I was terrified of the divine wrath that would come down on me. I was torn, driven hither and yon; in order not to be obsessed with her, I would strain to think of Sylvie, to whom I had sworn to be faithful.

Then, finally, once, we were alone together.

Unfortunately, my desire for Franca was stronger than my love for Sylvie, and I could not control myself.

Second floor, first door on the right, next to the emergency exit. I stood in that room with the other African brothers, with our Sunday clothes, our paddles in hand, and our good mood after lunch. Table tennis started Sunday at 3pm, and no one was to enter before that. We looked forward to this impatiently; it was the only time during the week when we could get together, have fun and chat lightheartedly.

That day, however, standing with my back against the door, I was watching the others play cheerfully and feeling sad.

"We must fight back!" I suddenly blurted out.

There was a silence, followed by laughter and comments such as, "Brother, you're crazy!", "No, no, brother, you are crazy! Don't you know it's very dangerous to go against these people?", "You are the latest arrival, and you still don't know Don Pietro! Your life now depends on him. Once you understand this, you will become more humble, brother!", "We need to train you before it's too late. You need a good correction, brother. We don't want to know where you got that fucking idea, but you need a good slap!", "Wake up; you're in Europe!"

"We must follow the dictates of reason," I protested, "and reason calls us to rebel."

"Says you?"

"That's right," I said, firmly.

"So, brother, you really need to be taught a lesson."

"Do you behave this way just because you are poor?" I asked out of the blue.

Suddenly, everyone was silent. I could only see bowed heads. I felt I had hit the nail on the head.

"Why do you have this attitude? Why do we tolerate being treated like starving people? Where is our dignity? Are we still under the Black Code? The Black Code of Slavery was instituted in 1648 in the French colonies and stipulated that slaves had no rights except to two and a half pots of cassava flour a week. Nothing seems to have changed since then."

"What are you saying?" they answered in chorus, defensively.

"I am saying that we are stupid! That we only act like house Negroes! Like scoundrels! Like fools! We hide behind our poverty to avoid taking charge of our lives. We prefer to be beggars, depending on the generosity of others! We act like sons of bitches incapable of doing something great and noble, generous or healthy. Something that can advance mankind! Our ancestors, the pharaohs, would curse us instantly!"

"Brother, enough! Who do you think you are, talking to us like this?"

"I am no one! The fact remains that we are just stupid, and we are enemies of Africa!"

"Shut up!"

"No, it is all our fault that since the end of the reign of the Pharaohs our continent has known only total intellectual and scientific darkness, total emptiness, becoming a collection of fifty-four ragged countries, however rich in gold, diamonds and oil... We are beggars seeking and buying weapons to destroy and kill each other. We beg for assistance from the West and buy sophisticated weapons from them. It is totally absurd!"

"Enough!"

"No. Open your fucking ears and listen to what I'm saying: we pray to a Western God; we beg for the mercy of a Western superpower; we let them call us 'fucking Negroes'. Slavery, colonialism and neocolonialism have made us imbeciles, strangers to ourselves and enemies of Africa. This is our reality. We seem to become intelligent, brilliant mathematicians, poets, writers, researchers, accomplished doctors, only if the West wants it and if we emigrate here. Let's stop sleeping and wake up!"

"Enough! Enough, brother!"

"Let's rebel!" I fiercely insist. "Let's rebel!"

This was not how I had imagined my life in the West, full of abuse and hardship. Yet, faced with the prevarications of that closed community, I felt that at last my life had meaning and that I had to rebel. Things had to change so that better times would come for me and my brothers. But, as I expected, the others were hesitant, wary. Suddenly their faces took on expressions of terror. I turned around and saw Don Pietro standing at the door, visibly angry, in a somber mood, holding the Bible at heart level as always. But I had a weight on my stomach, and I had to get rid of it. I was the only one in the room who did not feel annihilated by Don Pietro's omnipotence. I was getting used to not always looking back, not lingering in the past. After difficulties,

I had been able to recover and look forward with determination. That morning for the umpteenth time I had refused to participate in the eleven o'clock Mass. I was the only one who had not honored the Lord's Day, and I expected an outburst of anger from the priest. I had seen him slap some brothers several times.

The closer he came to me, the more I retreated, fearing that I would be slapped.

Don Pietro left the Bible on the ping-pong table, and I grabbed a paddle.

"Son, Jesus loves you; however, know one thing. If you are here in Italy, it is because I wanted it, and I can't stand you disrespecting me and our community. You won't be able to do as you please anymore!" said the reverend in a deliberately quiet and suave voice.

"My goodness, Father, I just want my freedom. Here we feel conditioned to accept all physical, psychological and spiritual abuse."

"You always have something to say. Behaving this way, it is not possible to make yourself a great man, an important person for Africa. If you commit yourself to go in the wrong direction, you can only go so far."

"Sure, this community that brainwashes us and teaches us to be servants!"

"You are a demon!"

"Why? Because I tell the truth? I guess you are our only hope, our only possible way to prosperity!"

"Jesus is love, my son. He loves you, even though you are a lost sheep. Pull yourself together and come back to me."

"I realize that you and I do not have the same views regarding social welfare," I replied, straining to smile.

"Listen to me, son. Listen to me well. No more arguing. My words are orders. You must conform to the rules of this community! From now on, you must show yourself as an exemplar, otherwise I will treat you like a wild African, and I may even expel you from our family and send you back to your jungle! Never again, I repeat, never again do I want to hear you question my orders!"

"Is that a threat?"

"That's right."

After dinner I left the dining room before everyone else and lay in bed brooding over what had happened, determined not to change my attitude. To change would have been a crime against myself. Lying in the dark, I wondered what the secret of a truly happy life was. My parents had worked hard, yet they had not achieved happiness and wealth. Don Pietro held the minds and spirits of us boys; I watched my terrified comrades and still couldn't understand why we were there. I dreamed of that very same respect that naturally comes to every man or woman born in a Western country coming to me and my brothers. And instead, here I was hoping that someone or something would grant me permission to live my life and achieve my ambitions according to who-knows-what principles. I was angry, but also very much disappointed.

I started having trouble sleeping well, and I had a hard time getting out of bed in the morning. I felt increasingly isolated and lived a monastic, monotonous existence. Fortunately, I was able to wake up early enough to study, because I wanted with all my heart to create a great future for myself. When I met Franca at the dinner table, the two of us would go and sit on a bench in the garden and I would express to her my conflicting feelings of fear and desire. Sometimes I would dream that, with luggage in hand, I would go through the gate and leave Don Pietro's unhappy community, but when I woke up I didn't have the strength to leave. Franca's presence relieved my loneliness, filled my inner emptiness. I was a castaway in a storm of doubt, and Franca was my savior. I had not made it clear to myself what the feeling was between us, but I felt that Franca was my anchor in a stormy sea.

"I want to leave the community, Franca!"

"Ah!" she sighed.

"I don't know how to tell Don Pietro."

"Be braver, love. Be yourself. Don't pretend to be happy if you're not. You have great aspirations and a bright future ahead, I'm sure."

She encouraged me to present myself as I was, with all my uncertainties, to become aware of my limitations but also of my abilities.

Every now and then I would close my eyes and imagine going where I wanted to go.

"Never forget that I can ruin your life; all I have to do is snap my fingers and…" Don Pietro's voice brought me back to reality.

"Do you know what you are? A bloody sadist who oppresses the poor! You only care about three things: money, power and so-called holiness."

"You're a demon!" he replied.

Finally, I met someone who helped me make up my mind.

That person's name was Matteo Scornavacca. I had met that boy, who was my age, during the meetings that Don Pietro organized to humble us. He always came with his parents, and the last time, during the gathering after lunch, I had told him about my difficult situation in the community. He, not knowing what contract bound me to the priest, discussed it with his parents, who proposed on the spur of the moment to accept me into their family. I therefore decided to leave Don Pietro's community, my only family in Italy. Any other place would be better than there.

So, one day, I walked down the long hallway to where the priest's office was located, tense with anxiety, my legs shaking. Arriving in front of his door, I knocked. "Come in!" I heard him say.

I entered.

Don Pietro was standing by the window behind the desk.

"Have a seat, son!"

I shook my head, no.

"I insist, son, sit down."

"No, I prefer to remain standing," I said. For a moment, there was only silence, but I knew it was a false peace, the quiet before the storm. He gave me an angry look, and I was seized with panic and began to tremble. I stared at him without speaking.

"Holy Virgin, but how taciturn, how proud, how damned surly you are!"

This remark, instead of upsetting me more, infused me with courage.

"Thank God I am a free man and I speak my mind," I retorted.

"You're a selfish, rude… demon!" the priest hissed.

"Why? Just because I don't want to live in this community anymore?"

Don Pietro sat down slowly, slower than a turtle. "Soon I will send you back to your country."

"But I'm talking about now, right now!"

"And where would you go?"

"I have an acquaintance in Milan."

"You know someone?"

"Yes."

"And you want to leave the community!"

"Yes."

"Be realistic, son. Think about your future; it is very important. I am your only hope."

"No. I'm leaving."

When you are born into poverty and another person takes care of you, you feel compelled to be grateful for your whole life, to obey them. Often you cannot see farther than the tip of your nose. The rich man almost always subdues you with charity and forces you to look only at the good he offers you. He exploits you at will, and you live in a precarious situation. The dependence you have on him seems almost like a perverse thanksgiving. There is no reciprocity; there is someone giving, and someone taking in return – only predation.

"You're crazy!" he said, and added sarcastically, "Good luck!"

I would be lucky, because I had chosen what to do for myself. And that would be fine, I told myself.

I walked out of Don Pietro's office with my head held high, and a week later I moved in with the Scornavaccas. They immediately offered me a bed in their house. Unfortunately, after a couple of days, I realized that those people had the same mentality as Don Pietro. It became clear when Matteo's father told me, "Normally, Don Pietro would have sent you back to your country. We, instead, are Christian, tolerant, and not so evil as to ruin your life." I had left my only home in Italy, my companions and Franca, for a losing bet with destiny. But I had to hold on.

31

Going to jail is not difficult, but regaining freedom is. The battle to prove my innocence will end with the hearing in nine days, acquittal or conviction.

I am in the gym with three inmates, working out on the benches with barbells. It is the time of day when my determination makes me invincible, or maybe the right way to put it is: I just don't give in. If there is any way to recharge with positive energy, this, to some extent, moves me away from boredom and pessimism; every second of my treadmill run reminds me of my freedom.

"Your real strength," the Prophet had taught me in Laa'Si', "is to know what you value most. You must always avoid being distracted by outside pressures that only fill you with doubt."

There have been many periods in my life when I have been plagued with doubt, but in time I have come to realize that there is such a thing as a healthy doubt, one that protects me from making a mistake out of rashness, preventing me from continuing down the wrong path. After all, only a fool has no doubts.

At that point, I wait until my instincts give me the green light to continue; that way I can focus on my real priorities.

The universe pushes me toward the best path to take by removing all hesitation. The road to my success seems to be interrupted by my imprisonment, but here in the gym I avoid being overwhelmed by negative thoughts that try to block and destroy my self-esteem. As I continue running on the treadmill, sweating and panting, my mind returns me to beautiful moments in my life with my wife. My mind wanders back to this summer; at six in the morning, three times a week, we would put on our sweatpants and sneakers and go for a run in the park.

We always took the same route; we would run for half an hour and then stop. I would go up to my wife and ask her to close her eyes with me. We would take a slow, deep breath, hold it for a long time and exhale slowly. Then we would do it again, more and more slowly, inhaling positivity and exhaling whatever was bothering us. When we opened our eyes, Hat always said, "Now I feel full of energy and I can face the day!"

The feeling of nostalgia for the memory of those precious moments is overwhelmingly heartbreaking.

Always, running on the treadmill, sweating and panting, I keep replaying in my mind the days with my family. Life is short, and each new day is supposed to bring us happiness. For me, Sunday has always been sacred, and I would spend it with my wife and children; sometimes in the morning we would go to church; sometimes we would have a picnic in the park, under a tree, communing with nature. During those picnics I would carve out an hour or so to be alone, to relax my mind and body.

"To give to others you must first give to yourself," the wealthy businessman taught me, "otherwise you will end up giving nothing to yourself, your family and your job. You have to know how to control time, because time is our life."

Now I am in prison. I am also at war against the system, against the prison gangs, against the racists. And they all seem like the same thing to me, the same entity. Some of them want to silence me by locking me up in jail, thus destroying me; others want to kill me. I am crushed by a system that once again constrains me and deeply undermines my resilience.

A sudden noise, a thud, brings me back to reality. I see one of the three inmates lying on the ground, his chest being crushed by the heavy barbell. I rush to rescue him. Blood drips from his mouth, and as I and others help him, he loses consciousness. Fortunately, the paramedics arrive in record time and take him to the infirmary.

*

This scene reminds me of the time when, as I was about to lie down under a tree to relax, I saw a young woman on the ground beside a bush. Her clothes were torn. She had one breast out; her red lacquered nails were dirty, her legs full of cuts and abrasions. Her blonde hair was long and shaggy. She was wearing heart-shaped enamel earrings and her nose was pierced and I could see she had a full sleeve tattoo on one arm. Her appearance made one think of one of the drug addicts who prostitute themselves to pay for drugs.

"Good morning, sister," I said. She did not respond.

"Good morning, sister!" I repeated, a little louder this time.

Nothing.

I felt her pulse: it was very low. Thinking she had overdosed, I grabbed the cell phone in my pocket and called 118. Kneeling beside her, I administered CPR. Suddenly the young woman took a breath, but her pulse was very weak and she could not respond to me when I spoke. She opened her eyes and looked at me for a long time. I understood that she was thanking me.

"Life is a gift from God," I said as I continued to hold her hand while checking her pulse.

She looked at me with wide eyes and gave me a faint smile of gratitude. I put my ear close to her mouth and she murmured, "My name is Silvia."

I heard the ambulance sirens and soon the rescuers reached us.

32

There is movement here, in the library; two people are occupying two of the three computer stations, and I am sitting with another inmate in the reading area. I am reading the newspapers in an attempt to get some useful information about my case.

The media portray me as a monster, a ruthless murderer that should be locked up in prison for life: "That thug killed an Italian woman and deserves to rot in jail!" and "Let's ask the judges for an exemplary sentence. Zero tolerance for criminals!"

The library door opens and the Italian and his three tattooed South Americans enter. This time the two Maghrebians are not there.

"Out!" orders the Italian.

The three inmates jump up and rush out.

"We are alone, Doctor," says the Italian.

"What are you doing here?" I ask.

"I wanted to save you the trouble of looking for me. I think you know what I want."

"I thought you understood that I made no such deal with you. I'm not paying for my freedom!" I assert forcefully.

"You either pay," says the Italian, "or I'll break all your bones right now!"

From outside come the sounds of an altercation.

A foreign voice tells someone that they cannot enter, but the door swings wide open and slams against the wall. Three men enter.

The first is young, between 28 and 30, wearing a black Yves Saint Laurent leather jacket worth at least 3,000 euros, Rokker jeans, Air Jordans on his feet. He has black, curly hair with a 500-euro haircut and a well-groomed patch of beard. He is tense, angry.

"Who the fuck are you?" the Italian asks. "How dare you—"

"Leave the doctor alone."

"And who the fuck are you? Leave now before we break your legs."

They do not respond.

"I asked you a question!"

They do not answer.

"Holy shit, now you're going to…"

The Italian tries to throw himself at one of them, but one of his South Americans grabs him by the arms and holds him back.

"Calm down, Boss," he says.

"Like hell I'll calm down!" the Italian shouts. "I'm going to smash these guys' heads in!"

"They're the Boss's men, Boss."

"Shit! Shit! Shit! All right. I don't want any trouble." The Italian shrugs his shoulders, as if to say, *"I can't challenge you!"*

There is a noise outside the door again. Shouting. Fists and slaps. Grunts of pain. More cries.

We see an angry inmate appear at the door. He enters and walks toward the Italian, who looks at him and arches his eyebrows.

"I came to tell you I'm done," he says. That voice reminds me of someone. "For me, the agreement is no longer valid. I'm not giving you another cent, and I expect you to leave me alone."

"You don't make the rules, you moron!" the Italian rants, pointing a dagger in his face. "I really don't think you are done with me."

With dexterity, the prisoner grabs the handle of the dagger and snatches it from his hand. Then he delivers three lethal blows to his face. I hear a clatter of broken bones and the Italian slumps to the floor at his feet.

The South Americans go to intervene, but the newcomer has already put his arm around their leader's neck and is holding the dagger to his throat.

The South Americans freeze.

"What the fuck are you trying to do?" the Italian asks.

"I'll explain how it works," says the other, whom I can finally identify. It is Gianni Pardini, the son of a bitch who swindled me a few years earlier. "I'm going to leave now and continue to live here in peace. If any one of you comes after me, I will kill you all. Understood?"

"Understood," the Italian replies.

Using the Italian as a shield, Gianni leaves the room.

No one moves; they just watch him leave without doing anything.

It is one against three, but no one will take the risk.

33

Gianni had been a friend and colleague of mine years earlier. At the time he needed a guarantor to get a 100,000-euro loan from the bank for a house. After a failed marriage when he was very young, he was about to marry Simona, a great emergency room nurse whom I met when I was called for gynecological emergencies. Gianni proudly showed me his future house, which was spacious and very bright. As time passed, Gianni's girlfriend also became someone I called a friend. The two of them often came over for dinner. Gianni was desperate to buy that house and urged me several times to sign a surety bond. Hat always advised me not to do so, because she did not trust a man with a poker habit.

"A guy like that always ends up screwing up!" she warned me.

But Gianni Pardini was someone everyone liked. Simona actually let slip that at night he played cards and liked to drink, but he was a serious and punctual professional. In the hospital they considered him the best surgeon in Milan, a smart one. Hat's negative opinion regarding Gianni's request resulted in me saying a hesitant no to him every time. And even when I made up my mind one night to say yes, I was not entirely convinced. But I felt at peace because I was helping a friend in his time of need. At the end of dinner, while the two women were in the kitchen washing and putting away the dishes and cutlery, and my children were in their little room, he asked me in a very kind tone for the umpteenth time in the name of our friendship to help him with that mortgage.

I did not immediately understand what was going on. The next day I went to the bank with Gianni and made myself guarantor of his loan. Unfortunately, I did not know at that moment that his life was on the brink.

Two years ago, Gianni told me that he had accepted a 'well-paid' medical executive position at another hospital on the outskirts of Milan. I was really happy for him but worried about Simona.

"And what is she going to do, stay and work with us in the emergency room?" I asked.

"No. She is coming with me and will work as my secretary and nurse in my private practice."

We said goodbye over lunch at a restaurant adjacent to the hospital. From that time on, we did not see each other again. At first, we talked by phone, but after a time, when one called either Gianni or Simona, one got the recorded message, 'The number you have dialed is not recognized.' This seemed strange to me; however, I was sure that sooner or later they would contact me. Well, I was wrong.

About a month before my arrest, my phone rang. The man on the phone introduced himself as the branch manager of Intesa San Paolo Bank and told me that he had some urgent information for me about Gianni's loan for which I was the guarantor. It could not be discussed over the phone; I had to go to the bank.

The next day at the bank, I was ushered into the same office where I had signed the guarantee, but the official was not the same one who had me sign. Without introducing himself the man signaled for me to sit down.

I said, "Good morning," and then asked, "Is your colleague not here?"

I expected him to answer, *"He's on vacation,"* or *"He's been promoted,"* or *"He's been transferred,"* but the manager, calmly ignoring my question, placed a newspaper, opened to the local Milan news section, under my nose. The article was about Gianni Pardini. He had gone to jail for fraud, and the bank needed to recover the remaining 100,000 euros of the loan I had gotten for him. I was the guarantor and had to pay.

"It's the law!" concluded the director.

My world fell apart. The bank gave me one month to inform them how I intended to repay that amount. I couldn't pay it all in one installment; maybe I could have spread it over six years, but I couldn't afford to shell out 1,400 euros a month, since I already had projects in the works, projects for which I had applied for other loans. I didn't know what to do.

Now, since the bank manager had given me the news that I had to pay the debt and could not tell me in detail what crime Gianni had gone to jail for, I needed to find Simona to find out exactly what had happened.

That afternoon I pressed the buzzer for the apartment Gianni listed on the mortgage application. There was no name on the intercom, no identifying information except the number 4, which I remembered was his.

I expected the intercom to be answered by an embarrassed and deeply apologetic Simona, but instead I heard a man's rather impersonal voice say that no Gianni Pardini had ever lived in that house. I insisted that it was the home of a surgeon friend of mine and that I had been there once.

When the man shouted, "This is my house!" and abruptly hung up, I was bewildered. I did not know how and where I could find Simona. I remembered that in the hospital cafeteria, I occasionally saw her with Silvia, a fellow nurse who seemed very close to her. I immediately went to the emergency room; fortunately, Silvia was on duty. She informed me that Simona had been estranged from everyone, especially Gianni, for a year, and was living with her parents in Vigevano. I went there and found a disappointed woman, looking tired, frail, prematurely aged. She was no longer the girl I remembered, that girl who was so full of life. She was a wounded soul.

"He ruined my life… I had to get away from him!" she told me as we sat on the terrace of her parents' apartment. She told me the whole story.

"He is a dangerous man. He never bought that house. What you actually signed was a surety bond to pay his gambling debts. The bank manager and the fake owner of the apartment worked for him, got him fake documents to get the fake mortgage that you guaranteed. He didn't do it just with you; he did it with others as well, and I didn't know anything about it. He confessed to me when the police came to search our house in Rozzano. They were looking for evidence, records of his scams! I was horrified. Was it possible for a great surgeon to be considered a fraud?

"He later confessed to me that it was a matter of life and death. He had become a slave to his gambling habit and would lose as much as 10,000 euros in a single night. To repay his gambling debts he had turned to loan sharks, who had forced him into drug dealing and swindling. The scam expanded into his private practice. I would make appointments and he would schedule surgeries for people who were perfectly healthy and then refer them to a private clinic, colluding with those in charge, thus defrauding both health insurance companies and the National Health System. They were well-organized, those criminals. So many decent people fell into their net. The bank manager was caught, fired and put under house arrest for fraud; two clinic managers and the fake homeowner were sentenced to ten years in prison for aggravated fraud. On the day the cops came to search our house, and my husband confessed to me that he was a criminal, I was so shocked that I didn't even have the strength to cry. Our marriage was dead. A week later I severed ties with him for good."

When I got home, I told Hat about Gianni, who, as it turns out, we did not know. Instead of scolding me, she wanted to make love to me, and we did so with overwhelming passion, barely stifling sighs of pleasure so as not to wake the children sleeping in the next room. Only later, tightly embraced, did we broach the thorny subject.

"What should we do? Maybe I should put my master's degree on hold…"

"No. Don't even consider it. That master's degree is going to enable you to advance in your career and also to better plan our project…"

"I have only paid the first instalment for this year, and…"

"It would be irresponsible to quit just now, when you are only six months away from finishing. I won't let you throw it all away. We will find a solution with the bank."

"You are right. We must not abandon our project. Have a little patience, Hat, and you'll see – we'll have lots of money!" I was trying to reassure her, but privately I had my doubts: things were not going as we had hoped.

"You are very clever, and you'll surely find a solution to this problem," my wife said.

"Unfortunately, apparently no one wants to trust me."

"Rest assured, we will get what we want!"

At the time, my wife had lost her job due to the economic crisis. The natural and organic cosmetics company in which she was an executive had had to declare bankruptcy and shut down.

However, I finally decided to ask for help from Roger, who, through his connections, convinced the bank to spread Gianni's debt payment over six years.

34

"It's useless for me to tell you that you're a son of a bitch, because you know you are! And sons of bitches don't change like that overnight!"

I am quietly reading a book when Gianni comes into the library to talk to me. He tells me he has been in solitary confinement for two weeks until the day before because of a fight with his cellmate. Gianni smashed the man's jaw with his fist. Now here he is, claiming he has changed.

"Ben, I ask your forgiveness for what I did to you…"

"Ahh, forgiveness!? Do you know I am still paying your debt?"

"I was at a loss, and—"

"Why don't you go to—"

"Take it easy, man. You don't need to remind me of my sins. I know them by heart, and I'm not proud of what I did to you."

"Yeah, I can imagine."

"How are the preparations for your trial going?" he asks.

Preparations? Why is he talking about 'preparations', as if my trial is a wedding? Prison has really made him lose his mind.

"Fine," I reply. "How do you know about my case?"

"I've read the papers; I've read up on it and I've talked to someone in here who knows everything about everybody – the Boss. What lead is your lawyer working on?"

"I don't have to tell you."

"The police don't just randomly accuse you of murder, you know."

"Listen, Gianni, I want to keep reading my book. Did you really come here just to bust my balls about how the police are proceeding with my case?"

"No, but… I know Inspector Trebano. We've never socialized but we have mutual friends."

"Am I supposed to believe you, after all the lies you have told me in the past?"

"Believe me, man. I really want to help you. Because of his gambling habit, Inspector Trebano ended up in the hands of the Mafia. My friend, who is also his friend, one with the dough, saved him a few months ago by paying off his debts."

"Generous of him!"

"Indeed. A true and generous friend."

"All right."

"I'll try to call him and find out what he knows about your business. However, I have to inform you that Trebano is a racist."

"He too!" Who knows why this no longer surprises me?

35

"Dr. Ben Kom is guilty of a heinous crime committed against that poor woman. I have no doubt that the court will convict him. Italy is a civilized country, not the African jungle! Criminals are punished here!" says Inspector Trebano, vehemently.

I am sitting in my favorite seat in the TV room. Our fearsome Trebano is being interviewed by an La7 reporter. According to him, all Africans are criminals.

"What a bastard! How can a policeman be so ignorant?" comments Diouf.

"If I wasn't locked up in here, I'd smash that creep's face in," says another.

Then the reporter interviews my lawyer.

"Dr. Ben Kom is not a criminal, but an upstanding citizen, a doctor who has delivered many babies and saved many lives. By the Hippocratic Oath he is committed to healing people; he could never kill. I have known him personally for years, and I guarantee that he can be trusted blindly. However, there is a criminal who has gone free, whom I will soon bring to justice. I will present evidence at the trial, which will end in my client being acquitted!"

When I leave the TV room, I find Gianni standing at the door.

"I've been waiting for you. Follow me," he says.

"Where?" I ask.

"Just follow me!"

I follow him in silence until we get to the bathrooms. Four inmates come out looking happy. Two are kissing while the other two are holding hands. Gianni enters the toilets and invites me to follow him. I hesitate. He insists. Finally, ruling out that he has turned gay, I decide to go in. And I am stunned to see two of them humping like it's nothing. Another pair of convicts enter and start kissing. Gianni pulls me by the arm, signaling me to disregard what I am seeing. In prison we indulge in behavior far removed from the life we would normally lead in freedom. Did I really have to get used to it? I didn't want to be there; I didn't have to be because I hadn't done anything.

36

"Suardi was the one who set your car on fire, and he will be convicted for it. He did not say why he did it, and during police questioning he never mentioned Monti's name," Andrea says.

"Monti seems unrelated to all this," I observe.

"Yes. However, I am continuing to investigate him."

"Who called the police?"

"I don't know yet. There also remains the mystery of who bought that phone in your name. But I will find out."

We are sitting in the prison interrogation room. I am very happy to again see my lawyer, who, in here, unlike in the visiting room, maintains a strictly professional attitude, since everything is recorded on camera.

"Trebano. What about Inspector Trebano?" I ask.

"Nothing. I haven't seen or heard from him for a week. He hasn't even sent the documents I have been waiting for…"

"He is a homosexual!"

"Who?"

"Trebano."

"Trebano?"

"Yes, Trebano! That's the one!"

"I didn't expect that."

"He has been seeing someone for two years, Andrea. And I learned that he is getting married abroad in three months."

"To whom?"

"To my colleague, Claudio Bianchi."

"Are you kidding?"

"Why would I joke about something like that? Claudio is homosexual. Gianni says he wants a gigantic wedding in Spain with hundreds of guests, but apparently Trebano has no intention of getting married."

"How does Gianni know all this?"

"I don't know. According to Gianni, Trebano always helped Claudio whenever he got into trouble – for example, he used to make Claudio's ex-wife's assault complaints disappear."

"Claudio was married?"

"Yes. He was, briefly. When she found out he was gay she immediately filed for divorce."

Andrea pulls out his cell phone and reads the messages. "It's my co-workers. They are following a lead."

"Meaning?"

Andrea explains to me in detail the information his team has dug up.

37

"Are you scared?" Mattia asks me, sitting on his bed, cross-legged.

I am walking back and forth in front of him. I feel helpless.

"Yes, I'm afraid of the sentence."

"If you can't prove your innocence, how do you imagine your future?"

"I don't know. Right now I don't know. Maybe I'll actually kill somebody in here so I'll have a justification for my sentence and feel I'm here for a reason."

"That's not like you, Doctor. You are a good soul…"

"Sure, yet it's hard to be a saint in here."

"Your trial is five days away. I ask you, are you still confident in your lawyer?"

"Yes, completely. You have to understand that Andrea is the best, and never disappoints his clients."

"Well, I also intend to continue helping you. What lead did you say your lawyer is following?"

Mattia is sincere when he says he wants to keep helping me. He knows my case as well as I do; I would say even better than I do. He reads every newspaper article about Barbara's murder. I explain that my lawyer and his associates were able to find the store where the cell phone and the phone card were bought in my name.

"Is Claudio really a homosexual?" asks Mattia.

"Apparently. I didn't know this until the day before yesterday."

"Is it he who is behind all this?"

"I don't know. Andrea and his staff are working to…"

"Sure. Though, you know, I know people who know other people…"

"You must not do anything illegal! I want to get out of here quickly and never have to come back."

He does not respond.

"I just have to call a friend today," he says. "It's all legal. I'll put him in touch with your lawyer."

"All right. Thank you."

"What do you seek in this life?"

Such a blunt, out-of-context question stops me in my tracks. Only one answer comes to my mind, "Nothing. I'm not looking."

"So, what is your goal in life?"

If I say I have no goals, I will not be telling the truth. Love, wealth and health are the important purposes of my life. However, when one begins to ask what the meaning of one's existence is, it is easy to get caught up in nostalgia. I close my eyes for a moment… And the drum show comes to mind…

*

My wife and I were in a theater in Milan attending an African show based on the sound of drums, which we learned about while searching the internet, unsuccessfully, for the meaning of the symbols embroidered on the cloth given to me in Laa'Si'. The theater was full, and the two of us were seated in one of the first few rows.

In Africa there are healer-hypnotists who heal using the sound of the drum, especially those suffering from nervous system disorders or insomnia. The sound of a healer-hypnotist's drum is pure melody; it is like a thermal water that you blissfully surrender to. This sound echoes within you throughout the day in a penetrating way, soothing you. A litany that heals the soul.

There was a loud banging of drums, then the low thunder of several drums as sun-like light radiated from the ceiling. *I must allow the light to penetrate me, into my subconscious, and follow the path it shows me,* I thought.

On the giant screen hanging behind five incredibly talented percussionists, fleeting images of an unfamiliar Africa appeared: portraits of prosperous, smiling people, beautiful landscapes, the skyscrapers of Johannesburg…

Then a circle of light illuminated a half-naked dancer huddled in a fetal position in the center of the stage. This was the allegory of the birth of the African continent. The dancer rose with graceful movements, leaving the shape of a heart in the artificial sand on which he was lying. It was Love triumphant.

The dancer shook his whole body to the syncopated

rhythm of a drum, evoking the essence of humanity and life.

A powerful voice, which must have come from the dancer's heart, repeated, "I am reborn in love! Because love conquers all things!"

The dancer was a great performer, an outstanding mime, and he was able, with his body movements and facial expression, to beautifully portray the feelings of loneliness and fear underscored by the rhythm of the drums.

Suddenly a radiant light, sunlight, blinded him, and he returned to the fetal position.

Then a dancer dressed as Nut, the Egyptian goddess of water, sky and night, entered the stage. Her steps were reminiscent of those of traditional dances. Lions, antelopes, giraffes, all the animals of the African jungle, ran happily on the giant screen behind the drummers as the dancer flailed about. The pace quickened; the dance became more rhythmic, wild, and the dancer seemed to enter a trance, establishing a spiritual contact with the goddess Nut. As I witnessed this amazing spectacle, I tried hard to find signs that deciphered the embroidery of Laa'Si'. But I could not.

38

Two days earlier, I received a phone call I did not expect.

"Ben, we can't see each other before the trial."

"What's going on?"

"I had a motorcycle accident a few hours ago," Andrea replied, breathing hard. "I was coming home after a tiring day at work, and at an intersection I was hit by a speeding SUV that didn't respect the right of way."

"I'm sorry; I hope it's nothing serious."

"I am in orthopedics with three broken ribs, and my left leg is fractured. I'm having surgery tomorrow."

"Everything will be fine, man. Just be strong. With a month of recovery and rest everything will be all right again. The problem is that I'm without a lawyer."

"Don't worry, Ben. I have instructed my team, and Sarah is a good substitute. She will come in my place to our next appointment."

Sarah is very young, in her mid-20s, a little more than

half my age. She is African and looks very well-groomed. Her hair is short, natural; she wears jeans and… she looks immediately familiar, like all the African women I have met – daughters of friends, girls who are my patients, someone I would have talked to on the street about school or my career. The guard who has escorted me in leaves us alone.

The lawyer stands up. We introduce ourselves and shake hands, then we sit down, and she starts talking.

"Doctor, I am very sorry…"

Before talking about the process, I feel the need to get to know her better. I look into her eyes and ask, "Are you Italian?"

"Yes, Doctor, I am Italian, but of Ghanaian descent. I was born in Milan."

"I suppose the white Italians respect you."

"In the eyes of most of them, I'm exotic, and some people act as if I don't exist. There are still a lot of racists out there."

"I know. But you have to… May I call you by your first name?"

"Certainly, Doctor."

"You must live your life. You are still very young, and if you have the courage to live your life fully, it will be magnificent. Tell me about yourself and your family."

"Three years after my birth, my brother was born, and my parents, who ran a small African food store, could no longer afford to live in Milan because life was too expensive, so they moved to Lodi, where the rent is much cheaper. We lived in a neighborhood full of immigrants.

Three years ago, having become an associate lawyer in Preti's firm, I answered an ad for a two-room apartment in Milan. I asked Preti, who has always supported me since I started my internship at his firm, to help me with the whole procedure, and so I got the apartment. On the day I moved in, the landlord shook Andrea's hand and welcomed him. Then he saw me arranging my suitcases in the room and got angry with Andrea, saying that he does not rent his house to African prostitutes. I was afraid that racist would never let me rent the apartment. My boss's reaction was exemplary. 'Are you trying to get sued for racism? Leave now, we are trying to move in!'"

*

I remember that I, too, at one time in my life was so afraid of losing everything – the support, food and shelter of Don Pietro's community. I was afraid of being repatriated.

Following my first meeting with Don Pietro, my passport and financial guarantee documents had been taken, and the money that my protector, the wealthy African businessman, had deposited in the bank for me had been withdrawn. Then they gave me a broom and a mop to clean the floors and the lawnmower to cut the grass in the garden.

We Africans need to know that, in keeping with the times, to build a future in which we are free we must have the courage to get out of charity-dependence, paternalism and condescension, which only destroy us.

In the community, I preferred to fantasize about my

rebellious thoughts on my own; and under the guise of studying, I would retire to my bed.

At night, I had begun to have a strange recurring dream. I dreamed I was an angel with big wings happily flying over a wide, sunny field. But when I looked down, I saw a man pointing a rifle straight at my heart. To save myself, I quickly flew upward, but he still managed to hit me, and I dropped to the ground, dead.

One night, I woke up after this dream and was sitting on the bed trying to interpret it, without much success, when I heard someone crying. I closed my eyes, convinced that that crying was coming from inside me, but upon realizing that it was not, I got up and followed the sound. At the staircase landing on the second floor, I found Ernestine sitting on a step, crying.

"Why are you crying, Ernestine?"

"I'm tired of living here."

"Why? They are so kind to take care of us poor people, don't you think?"

"At what price, Ben? They treat me like a slave even though I've been living here for five years. This is no life. I came to Italy to become a nurse!"

She told me that in her country she had lived on the streets because her mother had abandoned her. I wondered how she survived on the streets without family, without affection. Had she been raped? Had the poor unhappy girl been a baby prostitute? We spent two hours talking in the darkness of the staircase. We talked about the fact that she slept little and badly, about her unhappy childhood, about the day an old Italian priest found her in a state of malnutrition, fed her, urged her to convert to Catholicism and abandon traditional beliefs. And so she began attending church and serving during Mass. She was enrolled in the Catholic school in Kigali. And after many years at the mission, when she was 15, they promised to send her to Italy to study nursing because the priest's new dispensary was short of Western staff. Fewer and fewer Europeans were agreeing to come to Africa because of the starvation wages. Thus Ernestine was sent to Valsassina, and instead of sending her to nursing school, they sent her to the kitchen. Mama Ernestine – they called her that because no one cooked as well as she – never set foot in the classroom of a nursing school.

When she had finished telling her story, she burst into tears. I, on seeing a beautiful girl my age crying like that, was saddened and remembered how one time in the fourth grade, in order to console a classmate of mine who had flunked out, I hugged her, and she fell in love with me. With Ernestine I was undecided whether to stay and console her or leave after expressing my sympathy. The choice was difficult, partly because I did not want to find myself developing strong feelings for a girl other than Sylvie.

"Ben, I'm lonely," she sobbed. "Very lonely."

Her tears loosened the restraints of my caution and made me decide to put my arm around her shoulders. Immediately the poor girl rested her head on my chest.

"Don't worry; whenever you need me, I'm always here for you," I promised.

She calmed down and a beautiful smile lit up her face.

I stood up promptly and, satisfied, started toward my room, wishing her goodnight with my hand. She replied with another smile. Wonderful! As I was about to open my door, I turned in her direction and realized that she was still staring at me, and then she blew me a kiss with her hand.

*

"Never let others see that you are afraid. Never. Always remember that, Sarah."

"Yes, Doctor."

"Okay. Let's talk about my case."

"Oh Doctor, you will not be convicted of a crime you did not commit… We are working to get you out of here. I will help you."

I interrupt her. "Have you found the killer?"

"No, Doctor. But it won't take long. We know where the victim's lover lives, the man she dated from the Bunga Club."

"And did you question him?"

"We stopped by his house a couple of times, but he wasn't there. However, I investigated and found that they met only that night at the disco. Five days before the murder."

"Lovers for a night!"

"It would seem so. I am also investigating your gay colleague… Unfortunately, I can't find any connection between him and this affair. The morning of the day before yesterday, I visited him in the hospital to question him, and he was cheerful and smiling. He told me that it is absurd that we are suspecting him of this heinous murder. Later I will go to pick up the DNA results from the police. We finally managed to get the commissioner's permission, despite Trebano's objections. Then, tomorrow morning, I will follow up on the lead concerning the phone and the phone card registered in your name. We will get you out, I promise!"

"Thank you, Sarah. You have been really helpful."

39

We are in the interrogation room, and Sarah shows me a video clip on her cell phone. You can see an empty hallway. From time to time, a man or woman passes by to go to the bathroom. I can see Barbara's neighbor coming out of the women's bathroom, and a man entering the room on the opposite side. They get closer and start kissing passionately.

"But isn't that Barbara's lover?"

"Exactly. The footage is from two days ago. This is a hallway in the Bunga Club."

"It's clear those two know each other; maybe he's a philanderer who likes casual sex…"

"He must be. But not with the victim's friend. They have been dating for three years. We have evidence that he is the one who bought the cell phone and the phone card."

"But I don't know that guy. How did he get hold of my information?"

"I don't know yet, but I'm investigating. This asshole's

cousin is the owner of an electronics store, and that explains how he got those electronic gadgets, including the voice modification thing."

"He must be the killer…"

"We need evidence to nail him."

"Nevertheless… he does have the build of the man who attacked me and killed Barbara. Although I didn't see his face, it must be him."

"If it is him, he'll end up behind bars. Oh, shit!"

"What's going on, Sarah?"

"I have to go!"

"Where?"

"I have to follow your colleague, Claudio Bianchi. He's meeting Trebano in a café soon. Gotta go. I'll call you in the morning."

"And what do I do in the meantime?"

"Rest easy, Doctor. I know what to do to get you out of here," the lawyer assures me with a smile, then walks out.

An hour later, I go to the examination room. My wife is sitting at the table with a sheet of paper in her hand. It is not our weekly meeting day, but she has asked to see me. I smile at her.

"Hello, love," she says, getting up to give me a kiss on the mouth. "How did you spend your morning?"

"Hello, Hat. Just now I met the young lawyer—"

"Sarah, right?"

"Yes. There is hope with her."

"From the way you described her to me last time, I have no doubt. But do you know, it's strange…"

"What?"

"Yesterday, I received a phone call from one of your patients, the lawyer Dr. Angela Rossi. She asked me to come to her office immediately, but wouldn't tell me what it was about. I went to see her. She welcomed me kindly. Then she handed me a package containing information about one of her clients and told me to make good use of it. The woman is convinced that you are innocent."

"Did you open the package?"

"Yes. In it were bank documents with records of money transfers to different accounts in the name of a certain Vincenzo Taddia."

"That name doesn't ring a bell."

"What am I supposed to do with these documents? I don't understand."

"Since you can't bring them to me here, you should hand them over to Sarah right away. She will be able to make use of them."

"Of course."

40

"Sarah, I'm so glad to see you again," I greet her when she visits me again in prison.

"I took a big risk, and it almost got me killed."

"What happened?"

"Yesterday your colleague came to the café, as planned. Every table has a flowerpot. I was already sitting and reading the newspaper. He sat at a table a little way away from me and ordered a beer. As far as I knew, he had come to meet Trebano. Instead, another guy showed up, and he sat down next to Claudio. I quickly pulled out my tiny tape recorder, sneaked over while they were talking, left the device in a jar, unnoticed, then went back to my seat and pretended to read the paper.

"I heard a few mangled sentences: 'I'm terribly sorry, Claudio…' 'Holy shit, all you had to do was what I…' 'Come on, he's no longer an obstacle for you…' 'When I tell you to do something, just do it…' 'I get it…' 'Holy shit… Holy shit…' 'Give me a second chance…' 'No, I will never entrust you with a job again…'"

"Would Claudio really send that guy to kill me? And what did Barbara have to do with all this? He should have just killed me on the street, in the hospital, in my house – not another person's house."

"That is still a mystery, Doctor. Allow me to continue. Since he couldn't convince his colleague to trust him again, the guy stood up, speaking angrily. Then he suddenly stopped talking because he noticed the red dot of light on the tape recorder and realized that I was the one who had put it there when I approached them just a bit earlier. I thought he was going to attack me. I am a thin woman; he is much stronger than I, but I am strong enough to use pepper spray, which I always keep in my purse; so when I saw him approaching, I got up and kicked him hard in the nuts, then sprayed him in the face as he was writhing in pain. I ran away immediately. I'm glad I did.

"Until yesterday I knew nothing about him. When I got back to the office, with the intention of browsing the computer archive of the Milan court, I found your wife sitting in the waiting room. She wanted to hand me some documents. She and I did not talk much, but before she left, she said to me, 'Sarah, my husband trusts you.'

"I stayed in the office by myself and spent the rest of the afternoon and all night going through those bank documents, researching. I studied the transactions involving several accounts under the name of Vincenzo Taddia. I cross-referenced all the data I had and discovered that he is a former narcotics agent."

"Are we talking about the same guy you knocked out at the café?"

"Yes. He calls himself Rino. To investigate further, I phoned my fellow lawyer, who had given the documents to your wife. Fortunately, even though it was late at night, she answered me. This Rino terrorized Mafia families in Milan for a few years, then became one of them. I wanted to know more, but she didn't want to talk about it over the phone; she made an appointment for me for this morning at 7.30 in her office, and she gave me a very simple explanation: he loves the good life and beautiful women, so Rino allowed himself to be corrupted, as often happens to fragile souls. He was running around with a wealthy drug-dealing businessman who was also a hardened criminal. When he was kicked off the Force because he was giving drug traffickers confidential information about ongoing investigations or arrests, his Mafia friends put him in the money laundering business. He is cold, lethal and calculating. And although the police know he is involved in serious criminal activity, he has never spent a single day behind bars. Men like him strike fear into Lady Luck herself."

"Why?"

"Guess who Rino's uncle is?"

"If I don't know these people, how should I know?"

"Trebano. And it is he who has always protected his nephew."

"How did you get hold of this information?"

"I got it from my fellow lawyer – who, by the way, is Rino's lawyer."

"But doesn't lawyer-client confidentiality exist anymore?"

"Of course it does. But you helped that woman, Doctor, so she will be grateful to you for the rest of her life. The day she learned from the newspapers that you were accused of murder, she decided to help you prove your innocence."

"How?"

"By providing us with those documents that clearly show Rino's dirty business dealings, and especially the money – lots of it – that he received from your colleague, Claudio Bianchi. We also know that Rino made about ten transfers a few weeks before the murder, including two large sums: 10,000 euros to an electronic devices store, and 50,000 to a certain Malik Kunde, whom I don't know, nor do I know why…"

"Do you think that Malik Kunde had something to do with the murder?"

"I don't know yet, but I will look into it. The killer was very good, bordering on perfect. But, like all near-perfect killers, he surely made some mistake, and I will find it."

"I still don't understand how my patient was able to connect her client to all this."

"It's very simple really. It was during a conversation with her client, Rino. He is shallow, abject and arrogant. He had involved her in drafting a contract to cover up an illicit activity. That day he showed up in the office with his colleague, Claudio, and while my colleague was behind the desk preparing the document, the two of them talked about the job Rino was supposed to do. My colleague overheard your name mentioned, and these words: 'He has to pay… count on it… we don't need him alive… don't let me down…'"

41

It is Sunday. About twenty Catholic believers and I are at Mass in the prison chapel, listening to the chaplain's sermon.

"Only when we take 100 percent responsibility for all our actions can we turn our dreams into reality. God and His son Jesus Christ will empower us…"

When the rich businessman spoke to me about economic prosperity, he said that money gives power more than anything else. He clearly explained to me the main difference between a rich person and a poor person. He taught me the obvious truth that the rich man is free and his own master; he knows how to grow his money by having a long-term vision of what he wants to achieve in life; he creates work, earns, saves and invests to make money work for him. The poor man gets up in the morning with the sole purpose of finding employment if he has none, or going to work all day to earn a salary. The rich man thinks about wealth and gets it; the poor man thinks about poverty and gets it. This is the law: you become what you think about assiduously.

Right now, sitting on the pew with the other inmates, I am not thinking about my prosperity; I am thinking so much about my freedom that I feel as if I were going crazy. As the priest speaks, I shut my eyes. I am forcing my mind to reason, striving to be lucid.

First thing to consider: is Claudio really behind that murder?

Yes. Yes. Yes.

Secondly: what role does Barbara's neighbor play in this matter?

Sarah found out that, without knowing it, both women were dating the same man, a hustling Casanova. Barbara's neighbor is a drug addict; the drugs are supplied to her by Rino, who, taking advantage of his power over her, asked her to commit perjury as a witness against me.

But according to Sarah, this is a weak lead, certainly not leading to the killer.

Let's focus on the man who attacked me that night.

Thirdly: neither Monti, Suardi nor Claudio is the killer. That leaves only Rino.

Fourthly: what can I do?

I think back to how difficult it was for me to get an honors degree in a university environment where there were only about 20 African students. Even when people said there were too many blacks at Statale di Milano, I just smiled and kept pursuing my goals. Some people said the Africans looked as if they had just come down from the trees, or that they were savages.

Reaching my position in the hospital was even more difficult.

And now I'm locked up here in prison. For how much longer? Will I get out in time for the hospital competition? Is this the end of my career? I cannot allow Hat, Kemi and Naturi to live in poverty. I will never abandon them.

I have only one alternative: get out of here.

I remember the lesson the rich businessman taught me: to get out of difficulties, one must not run away but face them. *I am who I am, and I have victory within me.*

*

After Mass, outside the chapel, I find Gianni waiting for me in the hallway.

"Friend, can I talk to you for a moment?"

"I'm all ears."

"What did your lawyer find out?"

"That Claudio, my colleague, might be behind this," I reply, without mentioning the fact that he supposedly hired someone to kill me.

"I called a private detective friend the other day and asked him to investigate Barbara's life. And do you know what he found out?"

"I'm listening."

"That without knowing it, she and her neighbor were dating the same man."

"I know that."

"You also know that the bastard who calls himself Rino paid a bouncer from the Bunga Club to kill her?"

"No! They didn't want to kill her!"

"It doesn't matter if they wanted to kill you or her, I'm telling you that we are close to the solution."

"I'm not so sure."

"Don't be so pessimistic!"

"I'm not; I'm just trying to be a little realistic."

"The information I gave you is the key to everything; at least, one of the keys. It is the mystery from which everything that has happened unravels."

42

"I think I will go to the Bunga Club to investigate their bouncers. They might know something about that Malik Kunde, the one to whom Rino made the deposit. Thank you, Doctor, for the information."

"Don't thank me, Sarah; find the killer."

"I will!"

"I'll see you tomorrow at ten o'clock, Sarah," I say, but the young lawyer has already hung up. I remain for a few moments, staring at the phone I hold in my hand, while the joy of having someone as dynamic as Sarah doing her best to save me overwhelms me. I have a small glimmer of hope, imagining that maybe it is possible to get out, free myself from this situation. My family, my job, my career… maybe all is not lost.

*

The lasagna Bolognese is so tasty; it's the first time I've had such a good dish in this prison. I want a second helping, but in here, even if you're wolfishly hungry, they never give you an encore.

Sitting with Mattia, Gianni, Bacol, Diouf, Ousmane and Johnny at the cafeteria table, I eat and chat. My comrades seem nicer to me, and I feel really comfortable tonight.

"This lasagna is so good," says Mattia.

"Yes, exquisite," says Diouf.

"Tonight, they made it to celebrate the doctor's upcoming release. There are also pastries. In the two years I've been in here, I've never seen them before," Johnny adds.

"You are innocent, Doctor. They have no choice but to set you free. Remember us when you are out," Bacol says.

"Of course, I will. Thank you."

"Thank you for what?"

"You have taught me something, perhaps the hardest and most important lesson: you have to know how to trust others. You cannot always afford the luxury of doing everything alone in life. For this I will always be grateful to you all!"

The canteen door opens and in walks the inmate with the large Christian cross tattooed on his neck, the famous 'dickhead', the one the prison guards had warned me against dealing with. He approaches us with his usual grim expression.

"Really nice of you to join us," I tell him.

"Are you serious, Doctor?" retorts Mattia. "Do you really want him sitting at our table?"

"Yes."

"You know he cannot be trusted."

"I trust him."

"Jesus Christ, you're naive, Doctor! You've only been in here a little while, and you think that—"

"Who the fuck do you think you are?"

"A naturally better person than you!"

Dickhead does his best to remain calm. Seeing Ousmane's violent reaction, I feel compelled to intervene.

"I apologize on behalf of everyone. Sit down."

"No, he stays where he is, for fuck's sake!" rants Ousmane.

I am once again forced to calm everyone down and ask my friends to make room for the newcomer who sits opposite me.

"So," I ask him. "Did you do the thing you promised me?"

Dickhead clears his throat. Then he explains that his brother out there investigated Trebano through his connections and discovered that the latter, Claudio and Rino are part of a far-right Masonic lodge, of which Trebano is the leader. Skin color has always been an issue for them, especially black skin. They got together during one of their secret late-night meetings and decided to make me pay for my ambition to become a chief physician. Trebano said that night, "Better that that position goes to you, Claudio, or to one of us, than to that monkey!" And Claudio said I needed to be punished.

I listen attentively, asking him questions from time to time.

Claudio had said that I should be physically eliminated before the hospital competition. Trebano disagreed, but Claudio came out on top. Rino was in charge of making the plan of action.

43

My moments of solitude are the most intimate, anticipated moments of the day, when I finally lie in bed with my eyes closed. I am remembering a scene in the hospital with Silvia Brambilla, the girl I rescued in the park. I had promised to visit her in the ward.

I'm sitting on the small chair next to her bed and I ask, "How are you feeling?"

"Strange. Those people hurt me; they drugged and raped me for days. I'm stupid; it's my own fault… I shouldn't have…" she confesses to me, crying.

"Be brave, dear. Don't blame yourself for the evil they have done to you; they are cowards! Have courage!" I comfort her by holding her hand.

She has a sad expression. She is only seventeen years old. She is lying in a bed in the gynecology ward of the hospital, where I am on duty. Repetitive sexual abuse has deeply lacerated her private parts. Who knows if she will be able to have children? Who knows if she will have the courage to ask her parents for forgiveness for running away with a boy who she thought loved her? And what will her parents say when they learn that she has become a drug addict and a prostitute? Too late, she had realized that her father was right when he told her that she was too young to throw herself into the arms of a man to such an extent that she was willing to sacrifice everything for him. During that year, the poor girl lived through hell with the boy who had forced her into drugs and prostitution.

"I am happy that you trust me enough to share your fears and the story of your life with me. Don't be afraid, dear. Talk to your father, ask him for forgiveness, and you will see that he has never forgotten you. He has already forgiven you!" I tell her. The nurse enters.

"Good evening, Doctor," she greets me with a smile.

"Good evening, Giovanna," I reply, returning the smile.

"Hello, young lady. Did you have a good rest?" the nurse asks Silvia.

"Yes."

Giovanna takes her temperature and blood pressure. She then adjusts the dosage of the infusion, notes all the vitals and leaves. Soon afterwards, a young orderly brings a tray with breakfast, placing it on the bedside table.

"I have to go," I say, getting up.

"Uncle, you will still come to see me, won't you?" asks Silvia, wincing in pain while taking a sip of tea.

"Of course, dear!"

44

"We know who killed Barbara."

I had known Sarah would find the killer soon, but I remain silent, waiting for her to continue. It's just the two of us in the interrogation room.

"It was Malik Kunde. Take a look at this, doctor," Sarah says as she reaches into her purse and pulls out a folded sheet of paper.

I unfold the paper and see a picture of a big, muscular man standing behind Barbara's back as she is leaving the Bunga Club with Rino.

"It's from the footage that Andrea showed you on his phone. I reviewed that footage several times two days ago, and what interested me was the shot of the bouncer's torso just behind Barbara."

"Why?"

"Because of the gold chain around his neck with the Ankh cross hanging from it. Do you remember the killer wearing that chain?"

"Yes, of course."

"You can clearly see it in this picture. And then look at his right wrist," Sarah adds, placing another photo on the table.

"The gold Rolex!"

"Yes, Doctor, the gold Rolex. The bouncer behind Barbara is Malik Kunde, her killer!"

"How did you…"

"Yesterday I received a call: 'Dr. Sarah, can we meet? The time has come for me to speak.' 'Who is this?' I asked. It was 7.30 and I was in a hurry. When he told me that his name was Malik Kunde, I wondered why the murder suspect I was looking for was calling me, especially at that crazy hour."

"And what did he tell you?"

"Nothing. I pushed him to talk, but he wouldn't talk on the phone, and told me to meet him at 8.30 in a café on the outskirts of Milan, and asked if that was too early for me. 'No, no, no,' I answered. And he said, 'Good, because I can't hide anymore. They have tried several times to silence me. The time has come to tell what I know before it's too late.'"

"And did you meet?"

"I was standing in front of a shoe store when I heard someone approaching me from behind. I turned around, and standing before me was an African man, who said, 'Dr. Sarah? I'm Malik Kunde. Follow me; I have a confession to make.'"

"And you followed him?"

"He took me to a café down the street, and we sat at

a secluded little table and ordered two coffees. 'So, Malik, why are we here?' He told me that if he felt compelled to talk, it was only because he was very worried for his life. I urged him to tell me the whole truth and he confessed that he had killed Barbara with the help of her neighbor."

"How?"

"Three days before the murder, Malik went to her neighbor's house with his prepaid disposable cell phone and electronic voice-altering device, just to finalize some details of Rino's plan. Then on the second day he was there, at dinner, he told the neighbor that Barbara was dating Rino. The woman, jealous, became furious and told Malik that she wanted Barbara dead.

"The night of the murder, Barbara returned home from work at about 10.30, and shortly afterwards Malik knocked on her door. Since they knew each other, Barbara opened it and Malik went inside with a black gym bag. Barbara left him in the living room to go to the kitchen for tea, and when she returned Malik was dressed all in black and holding a ski mask in his hand. Then he made her call you, Doctor. And you know how that turned out."

"I still don't understand why he didn't kill me!"

"I asked him the same question. He replied that the call from the number registered in your name was Rino's Plan B, to still knock you out of the game if something went wrong or if somehow you didn't take the bait. Malik said that when it came time, he couldn't finish the job because you are an African brother, and he didn't feel like killing you. So, he made the phone call."

"Did you have him arrested?"

"No. I didn't have the time. I suggested that he go and turn himself in to the police, but immediately after the confession he ran out of the café telling me that he wanted to leave Italy. The day before, through some investigating, I had found out where he lived, so I went to the commissioner and told him the whole story. In the afternoon they went to his place, but unfortunately they found him hanging in his living room."

"Damn it!"

"That's not all. The commissioner then gave the order to find Rino. At 3am, a police helicopter went to his house; they lit it up brightly and with a megaphone ordered him to come out with his hands up. A dozen police cars had surrounded the place. I was there too; I saw everything. Rino approached the window, showing that he was holding a gun against Barbara's neighbor's neck. At that point policemen broke a windowpane and went inside; I heard a gunshot and saw Rino falling to the ground. They had hit him in the shoulder, rendering him harmless."

"What happens now?"

"Today the judge signed an order for your immediate release, and as of tomorrow you are a free man."

"Thank you, Sarah!"

"My pleasure, Doctor!"

"Call me by my name, Sarah. We are friends now. You are my sister. I need to meet your family."

45

I am sitting at a table in an African café in Corso Buenos Aires and I see Andrea coming, walking with a cane. I stand up.

"How are you, man?" I ask.

"Not bad, Ben. I'm in physical therapy, and it will take me about a month to be able to walk without a cane. How about you? How do you feel being out of jail?"

"I've been free for three days… I feel weird, but in good shape. Where's Sarah?"

"She's working on another murder case."

"Already? I thought she was going to take a break and come to lunch with us."

"Well, that was the plan, but what can you do? Work takes precedence. When is your competition?"

"In two weeks."

"Are you ready?"

"Yeah, I'm a little tired, but everything will be fine."

46

Two months later

I see on my cell phone that it's 5pm. I was in the operating room until 3pm, and since 8am I've done four surgeries, then sat at my office desk and gone over the patients' charts.

Roger and I are meant to be meeting for an aperitif just before 6pm. If I don't hurry, I'll be late. I send my friend a message on WhatsApp: *I'm still in the hospital. We're going to eat vegetarian, right?*

After a minute, Roger responds: *Of course! I'm parking the car in front of the café. I'll be waiting for you!*

I turn off the computer and get up. I take off my white lab coat, pick up my bag, and walk out to the subway.

I arrive at the café-restaurant at 5.35pm and find Roger settled at a table on the terrace. He has ordered a non-alcoholic cocktail. We hug each other.

"Sorry I'm late."

"It's okay."

I sit down and raise my hand to get the bartender's attention. My cell phone rings. I read: 'unknown caller'.

I pick up, "Hello?"

It is a patient who wants to thank me for the surgery I performed on her two weeks earlier, and especially for her regained health.

"Thank you; I'm pleased to hear that you are well," I say.

When the bartender arrives, I also order a non-alcoholic cocktail. As soon as he walks away, my cell phone rings again. It's another patient thanking me and asking for advice.

"I am always impressed by how much your patients love you," Roger remarks after the call.

"I am chief physician now, remember that. Anyway, I'm really very happy when they regain their health."

"Why are we here on Earth if not to give happiness to others? Do you remember when we dreamed of having everything that we have now?"

"Yes, I remember. You used to say that you hoped one day to achieve prosperity."

"And you kept pointing out that saying 'I hope' or 'I wish' inevitably leads to defeat."

"Sure. In Laa'Si' I was taught that the correct way to state our thoughts is to say 'I am'. If you say, 'I am prosperity, wealth, health, love…' with conviction, you will have prosperity, wealth, health, love in your life, because you will have set yourself up for the concrete realization of your goals; however, you have to believe in it with all your soul. If you want love, you have to give love to others: the more love you give to others, the more you receive. If you do not give, you cannot receive."

47

After the aperitif with my friend, as I am making my way to the subway to head back to the hospital and retrieve my car, I come across a very unfortunate scene. An African man approaches an elegant Italian man to offer him goods (newspapers, lighters, necklaces).

"Holy fuck, get lost!" says the Italian in a harsh voice.

The man insists, wanting to sell him a good luck charm, and the Italian sends him packing.

I immediately approach the young man and buy a newspaper; an old lady buys a bracelet; then he offers a young couple passing by a necklace.

"Leave us alone!" the man violently chastises him.

"It's a necklace for your woman, my friend."

"Friend, your ass!"

"But—"

"Fucking immigrant! Back off, you fucking peddler!"

The woman smiles contentedly at her partner, kisses him and caresses his back.

In the hospital's underground parking lot, I retrieve my car, which promptly gets stuck in rush-hour traffic. My phone on the dashboard rings. I take my right hand off the steering wheel so I can answer.

"Hello, Sarah, how are you?"

"Fine, Doctor, I can—"

"Sarah! What did I say to you the last time we saw each other?"

"I'm sorry, Doctor, I have so much respect for you it's not natural for me to call you by your first name. Anyway, I can confirm the dinner with my family. Tomorrow at eight. Is that okay?"

"Perfect, Sarah. We'll be waiting for you."

48

The next day, at seven in the evening, I wrap up 'Health Wednesdays', the weekly session I hold with patients and hospital visitors, with these words: "One must take the time to continuously renew oneself. The right food, the right amount of rest, relaxation and regular exercise keeps our bodies healthy. Spiritual renewal requires time for meditation, reading, music, and anything that brings us inner peace. The spiritual dimension encapsulates our value system; it is our center that releases and multiplies energies. We must acquire the habit of reading good books; this enables us to develop a mental dimension rich in positive experiences. True principles and values lead to peace of mind. We can renew our social and emotional dimensions only if we devote ourselves to others with integrity and unconditional love."

The hospital hall is full. After my talk, a lady in her 60s walks up and compliments me. "Well done, Doctor. Again, I liked what you said."

While the woman is still talking, an elderly man, more or less in his 80s, approaches, stating that he has something important to tell me. I ask him to wait a moment because I am still in the middle of my conversation with the lady. When I finish, I invite him to speak.

"Thank you, Doctor. My name is Giuseppe Brambilla. I used to be an entrepreneur. I am a lucky man; in my sixty-plus years, I have created a finance empire. Some of my fortune already supports so many people. I don't know how I will ever be able to repay my debt to you. You saved my granddaughter Silvia! Yes, you got it right. I have a foundation that focuses on health protection, and I would like you to work with us. You are a special person, and I would like to offer you the position of president of the Brambilla Foundation. I am very serious. Every health project that you support anywhere in the world will be funded by the foundation. Therefore, please accept my proposal!"

That offer fills my heart with joy, and when I step into my studio to pick up my bag and return home for dinner with Sarah's family, I stop in front of the canvas hanging on the wall. I look at it, but I don't see the two drummers beating on the drum or the man rescuing a wounded man. All I have before my eyes is the teaching of the sages of Laa'Si': we must believe in our dreams and help others, whoever they may be, with love and dedication, and our lives will take the right direction by themselves.

49

The guests have arrived on time. We are all dressed in African clothes. Sarah's mother, a beautiful woman in her 50s, wears an elegant, long evening gown with gold embroidery that shows off her shoulders. Her younger brother wears a black suit with a matching embroidered shirt. Her father, 55 years old with a slightly grizzled beard, sports an elegant traditional men's suit. Sarah is dressed casually, wearing a long-sleeved African sheer embellished with rhinestones. My wife looks beautiful in her high-necked dress. And Naturi and Kemi look adorable in their African clothing.

The table is loaded with various seafood dishes and the national dish of Cameroon, which is *ndolè*, a stew of shrimp and meat plus bitter herbs and peanut butter.

"Thank you for accepting our invitation to dinner."

"We are very happy to meet your family, Doctor," Sarah's father replies.

"Hey, Dad, remember when you first came to Italy and

some Italians were attacking you with racist epithets?" asks Sarah.

"Of course I remember, my daughter. That was the year the first African made his debut in the Italian Serie A championship. His name was François Jean Zahoui, and he was from the Ivory Coast. Why do you ask?"

"Because Italy hasn't changed, that's why. Mario Balotelli is constantly being insulted in the stadium; they throw banana peels at him…"

"One day some Juventus fans shouted in chorus that a 'negro' should not be allowed to play for the national Italian football team! According to them, a black man cannot be Italian!" adds Sarah's brother.

"Racists have mental problems. We need to defend ourselves against them without letting their hatred infect us. If we are united, we can express much love and defeat hatred. We can become anything we want if we don't set ourselves limits and constraints," comments Hat.

"These are all nice words, but it would be preferable to live in a different world," says Sarah. "They make us feel poor just because we are African and have black skin. The pages of newspapers are full of advertisements about these Western paternalistic charity programs for Africa. On television they show millions of people organizing marches to promote the culture of aid. The fight against poverty is propagandized through the entertainment industry by jet-setting celebrities, movie stars, rock legends, Christian churches, multinational corporations, governments, etc. Efforts are always made to help Africans in every way possible, yet we are sinking deeper and deeper into poverty doing it this way. What should we do?"

"It's simple, Sarah," I reply. "Only those who are rich can help those who are poor; the opposite is impossible. The poor man always asks, and the rich man gives. All our misfortunes come from our way of thinking."

"What does that even mean?" asks Sarah.

"For example, if we were in a town square and we asked people if they wanted to earn money, the answer would depend a lot on where we were. If we were in America, in Australia, in Canada, in England, 99 percent would immediately say yes, while in Italy only 60 percent would answer yes. In Cameroon, Senegal, Mozambique, the percentage would drop to four percent. Why such a disparity? Perhaps religion has something to do with it? Or fear? Is it a cultural fact? It certainly has absolutely nothing to do with destiny. It just depends on the way the question is phrased. In countries with the lowest percentage of people aspiring to earn money, it would be more appropriate to ask, 'Do you want to get out of poverty?' I am sure that 100 percent would answer yes. People have become so familiar with 'development aid', 'poverty alleviation' and 'missionary work' that they are ashamed to talk about money, or even to think about it. Being paid, aspiring for personal growth with even a modicum of ambition, is now seen as an act of defiance, of pride. But let's face it – no one likes being poor. Here's the secret! Instead of trying to change the idea of poverty imposed by the powers that be in the society you live in, you simply have to redirect your mind to a different way of thinking and direct your emotions toward wealth. 'You must strongly embrace a new life, and only when you are 100 percent responsible for your choices and actions will you see that you will achieve wealth,' a rich businessman told me."

"But it is the Westerners' fault that we are in this situation!" protests Sarah's brother.

"I understand you, but constantly blaming others for everything that happens to us can only make us pessimistic," I reply.

"I am pragmatic. What future would you and our parents have had if you had stayed in Africa?" he retorts.

"That's no excuse, son," his father asserts. "In Africa, at the time, our generation lived only with the hope of being able to study or work in Europe. Nature offered us the resources to achieve our prosperity in abundance, but for us, Europe was the only chance of becoming something in life. For me, Italy was a lifeline because I had always been fascinated by the Beautiful Country's culture, fashion, and football tradition. I had read so many magazines about the beautiful life Italians lead, watched numerous television broadcasts about the rich with their luxurious villas and nice cars, and I had drawn the conclusion that Italy was paradise. You, the youth of today, have not experienced colonization and neocolonialism the way we have, and you have so many opportunities to end the habits and beliefs of the past and begin to think correctly."

"You're right, Dad," Sarah says.

"You must know the truth, because knowing the truth leads us to act with confidence and security, gives unparalleled satisfaction. It is the only certainty in a world plagued by doubt and danger. To know the truth is to connect with an indestructible power that knows how to dispose of all errors, doubts, disharmony and contrast. Truth is humble and always triumphs! Before you were born and became what you are today, many black people invented things that contributed to the prosperity we enjoy today. I think of Lewis Latimer who invented the elevator, the first carbon-filament incandescent light bulb and the parallel circuit that keeps all the light bulbs in a house from bursting if one fails; Garrett Morgan who invented the gas mask, which protected many soldiers against chlorine gas vapors during World War I, as well as the first electric traffic light; Granville Woods, who invented a device that sent messages between stations and moving trains, making public transportation in the United States safer; Georges Speck Crum, the inventor of potato chips; Patricia Era Bath, the inventor of the laser device to treat cataracts – her invention has restored the sight of so many people around the world; André Rebouças, who invented the first self-propelled torpedoes for ships; Philip Emeagwali, who certainly contributed to the advancement of technology by designing the super-computer; and so on. These are just a few examples among hundreds of inventors of color..."

"The advice we give you as parents," Sarah's mother added, "is to live to the fullest without the fear of dying tomorrow, but with balance and self-knowledge in order to achieve immortal accomplishments. Never act in life like a poor beggar who reaches out his hand in front of a church, and thinks only of his next meal. The fear of poverty destroys those who carry it in their subconscious!"

I can only agree with Sarah's mother, yet even today many young people of African descent struggle to understand, to fully comprehend, how much of a difference they hold in their hands, and that they have the ability to transcend the conditions that have been inflicted on us. I still remember when I invited my peers at Don Pietro's to stand up, and they said no, terrified. Today we cannot any longer succumb to such fears.

50

"Fucking Chinese! Just think, Doctor – the whole world is in quarantine because of them," says Prof. Rossi, speaking in a disgusted tone behind his surgical mask as I remove the thermometer I had slipped under his armpit a few seconds ago.

"Thirty-eight point five, professor. How are you feeling? Are you dizzy?"

"A little… Here, you either die of coronavirus or suffer from loneliness. This fucking pandemic has disrupted habits that seemed immutable here in the West."

Trembling, he tries to lift himself off the bed.

"It is a lonely experience that we all go through, and it is no one's fault."

"Believe me, Doctor, it is the fault of those filthy Chinese, a population that has been taught from birth to obey rather than think!"

He manages to sit on the side of the bed.

"You are racist!" I tell him.

"No I'm not. I'm just telling the truth. They don't know what democracy is and they will never be like us!"

"You are racist!" I repeat.

"I am not racist, Doctor, you know that very well. If I were, do you think I would have allowed you, a black African, to come into my house and examine me?"

"I am here mainly because you need me. You have no relatives or friends. No one! And your illness is causing you a lot of suffering."

Professor Rossi is a retired university professor who taught history at the Università Statale di Milano. He was diagnosed with prostate cancer and had surgery a month ago. He has been my neighbor for about ten years, has no children and is unmarried.

"It's not like that, Doctor. You are different from other foreigners, and I have a lot of respect for you... Our life was running smoothly; nothing foreshadowed what happened in Italy and the world," he says, pointing to the TV set. Then his gaze becomes focused. "Let's hear what these bastards have been up to!" He turns up the volume. You can see the head of the Civil Defense Department, Angelo Borrelli, announcing the daily news bulletin, which shows the same devastating data.

"It's a war! And they are going to kill us all, us old people! We are dying because of the wretchedness and ignorance of these Chinks, who also invade us with their counterfeit goods."

According to the professor, who is a right-wing extremist, Italy is going down the drain because of others. For the past two decades, he has been in the forefront against a *jus soli* law. Italian citizenship law is among the most backward in Europe, being based on *jus sanguinis* (right of blood): a child is Italian if at least one of the parents is Italian, and if one is a foreigner, one can apply for citizenship only when one comes of age.

Professor Rossi is a fascist, yet I help him, since we live in the same apartment building. The first few times he saw me he avoided me like the plague, and when I greeted him he would turn away or lower his gaze, pretending not to see me, ignoring me completely.

Then one day he fainted coming out of the elevator and I was forced to rescue him before the ambulance arrived. At the hospital they found a tumor in his prostate and operated on him. Now that he is recovering, he needs me and calls me often during the day to check his vitals, check his dressings, and chat; always, of course, while wearing his surgical mask. Right now, I am examining the scars on his lower abdomen.

"It's healing nicely," I say, satisfied.

"Thank you," he replies. "Doctor... there is something I have to tell you."

"Yes?"

"We Westerners carry the burden of an enormous responsibility for the world. But you know, Doctor, I have my weaknesses but I am not a racist. I'm a generous man; for the past three years I have been long-distance adopting two African children, who are receiving an education because of me!"

51

After a night on call that I would describe as worthy of *E.R.*, more or less as usual, I find myself in the café in front of the hospital. It is half past eight. It is a particularly hot and dry June morning. Before going home, I treat myself to a cup of coffee. All the colleagues I meet shake my hand; some of them smile, greeting me with friendly pats on the back. The barman recognizes me immediately.

"Dr. Kom, what shall I get you? Coffee? Do you want Moroccan?"

"A cappuccino; I'll have it at the table." I take the cup, filled to the brim, and sit down.

I open my cell phone. There is a picture of my wife smiling. I send her a message on WhatsApp, then lock the phone. I am tired, but my mind wanders. I close my eyes and for a moment I feel overwhelmed by the weight of my effort to fit in.

I remember when I was a guest of the Scornavacca family, I always felt the strangeness of their relationship with me. Conversations at the table always revolved around my miserable existence as an African – racist subject matter. On those occasions I spoke very little, listened, and looked around the elegant apartment in San Babila. I had to suffer in silence, but inside there was a fire.

Not knowing anyone in Milan, I was completely dependent on the generosity of the Scornavacca family, who didn't care about my feelings. They had me eat great food but treated me as if I were a homeless, starving beggar. Matteo's mother, petite and always tanned, would say to me at the table, "Eat, eat, there's plenty for you too!" Her son's words cut like a knife, "Do as my mom says: eat. With us you'll never go hungry!"

It was really difficult for me to live in that house, but what interested me most was passing the medical school entrance exam. Even though they were racist, I had to accept them for what they were and endure it. I was brave, ambitious and resourceful. The closer I got to the day of the state medical school entrance test, the more convinced I became that I would pass it, and I was eager to meet my future classmates. Every morning I told myself, "There is no alternative. I am all alone in Milan. I have no family here and I have to get in!"

The test was made up of logic and science questions that I had studied well. There were 600 places available, and I was one of the winners out of 2,500.

If I had been in a better economic situation, I would not have chosen to spend a single day with the Scornavaccas, but even after I was admitted to medical school, I stayed with them for a month until I moved into the university dorms, where I shared a double room with Roger.

"Ben Kom!"

I open my eyes and see an obese man standing in front of me. He reminds me of someone. "Is it he or isn't it?" I wonder. He is smartly dressed, his well-made shoes holding up all of his 110 kilos.

"Luigi?" I whisper.

"Yes."

Ah, Luigi! Luigi Vota! That big bastard! We were friends for a long time when we were students in medical school. We even studied together. Then when we graduated and I did my residency, he moved away. When we saw each other again at a competition for a medical executive position at the hospital, he turned out to be a racist of the worst kind!

I remember the conversation we had at the end of the competition, when I told him about the difficulties I had fitting in.

"Why do you want at all costs to stay in my country, Ben? We have accepted you so far. We have trained you. You don't belong here. Why don't you go back to your country?" he said, harshly. "Here you will never become someone. Can't you see that you are different from me? Because this country is only for people like me, who physically look like me."

"I don't like what you are saying or your tone."

"I don't give a damn whether you like what I'm saying or not. Italy has given you far too much freedom, and now you have to leave. You have to go back to your home to help your people. You are not welcome here!"

"Are you trying to hurt me, friend?"

"Friend? You come here and steal our jobs and call me friend? Shit, Ben, don't ask too much of us."

"I have principles and goals that I don't—"

"Fuck your principles and your fucking goals! You are African and you need to go and help your people in Africa. Do you understand that or not?"

"Do you realize the gravity of what you just said to me? Be aware that you have ruined our friendship."

"I don't give a damn about our friendship!"

"You scare me."

"There can be no future for you in my country!"

"You are an asshole. I have ambitions as much as you do."

His words were like a stab in the heart. Today, after 20-something years, here before me stands Luigi Vota!

"You look good, Ben!"

"Thank you. What are you doing here?"

As I drum my fingers on the coffee table, his reply hits me like a rock.

"I am the new chief of orthopedics at the hospital. I heard you are chief of gynecology. By the way – congratulations!"

"Thank you. You too."

Silence. He had never been so gentle toward me. It bothers me to know that the two of us work in the same hospital. Even as a student, the bastard always knew he was going to have a career: his father was the director of the orthopedic residency school at Università Statale di Milano. He told me that I should go back to Africa, to help my people, but he had not been able to admit that his job was the result of nepotism and corruption.

I don't really know what to do. Maybe I should leave. He takes care of it, breaking the silence.

"Are you happy with your career?" he asks with a smile on his face.

Color me impressed. The very man who told me that this was not my country, and that choosing to stay here would take me nowhere, is taking an interest in my career.

"Yes. Why?"

"Just that. Simple curiosity really."

"Ah!"

"I have a nice family. I guess you do too. This weekend we are going to the sea, to the Marche region, where we have a vacation home. How about coming there with your family? It would be my pleasure."

"Really?"

"Really."

"I'm sorry, Luigi. That is not a good idea."

"It wouldn't cost you anything. You would be my guest."

"I'd rather not, thank you."

"Please…"

"I'm not in the mood to do you any favors. I have just seen you again after so many years and…"

"Come on, Ben. I'm doing this because of our old friendship; I—"

That excuse hurts me. Quickly I interrupt him, "Please don't say anymore!"

Luigi lowers his eyes. He seems tempted to add

something else but gives up. I take a last sip of my cappuccino, then get up and leave. If nothing else, Luigi has a somewhat relative concept of friendship.

This book is printed on paper from sustainable sources managed under the Forest Stewardship Council (FSC) scheme.

It has been printed in the UK to reduce transportation miles and their impact upon the environment.

For every new title that Troubador publishes, we plant a tree to offset CO_2, partnering with the More Trees scheme.

For more about how Troubador offsets its environmental impact, see www.troubador.co.uk/sustainability-and-community